Streiker's Morning Sun

ROBIN HARDY

NAVPRESS ●
BRINGING TRUTH TO LIFE
NavPress Publishing Group
P.O. Box 35001, Colorado Springs, Colorado 80935

The Navigators is an international Christian organization.
Jesus Christ gave His followers the Great Commission to go
and make disciples (Matthew 28:19). The aim of The
Navigators is to help fulfill that commission by multiplying
laborers for Christ in every nation.

NavPress is the publishing ministry of The Navigators.
NavPress publications are tools to help Christians grow.
Although publications alone cannot make disciples or
change lives, they can help believers learn biblical disciple-
ship, and apply what they learn to their lives and ministries.

Library of Congress Catalog Card Number:
    94-24299
ISBN 08910-98763

Cover illustration: Bill Farnsworth

The quotation in chapter 11 is from *Sifted But Saved* by W.
W. Melton. The Scripture quoted in chapter 14 is from *The
Message* by Eugene H. Peterson, copyright © 1993, used by
permission of NavPress Publishing Group.

"My Faith Looks Up to Thee" by Ray Palmer, 1808–1887.

The stories and characters in this book are fictitious and
any resemblance to other individuals is coincidental.

Hardy, Robin, 1955–
    Streiker's morning sun / Robin Hardy.
        p.   cm. — (Streiker saga)
    ISBN 0-89109-876-3
    I. Title.   II. Series: Hardy, Robin, 1955–
Streiker saga.
PS3558.A62387S85   1994
813'.54—dc20   94-24299
                                                    CIP

1 2 3 4 5 6 7 8 9 10 11 12 13 14 15 / 99 98 97 96 95

Printed in the United States of America

To gifted musician, composer, and friend
Renée Johnson—
thanks for the song

Other books by Robin Hardy

Chataine's Guardian
Stone of Help
Liberation of Lystra
Padre
Streiker's Bride
Streiker the Killdeer

Prologue

Our story[1] begins with Adair Weiss working as a teller at a bank owned by the reclusive Dallas billionaire Fletcher Streiker. One October day she is called into the office of the bank president and handed a file folder full of articles, letters, and other bits of information regarding the mysterious Mr. Streiker—but no photos of him. Adair is told that Streiker wishes to meet her, on one condition: she must agree to marry him sight unseen.

After grappling with this strange condition, Adair agrees. The ceremony is performed without Streiker, but when Adair finally meets him, she finds him to be the literal fulfillment of all her dreams. They spend one satisfying night together as husband and wife before he is called away again on urgent business. Before he leaves, he promises her he will stay in contact and return soon.

Although hurt and baffled by his departure, Adair

must follow through on tasks he leaves for her that seem senseless or humiliating. Because of his demands, she is unable to pursue ballet, her one great desire. At this time she also encounters an old enemy of Fletcher's named Darren Loggia who is trying to get to Streiker through her.

Loggia crashes a party Adair is attending and terrorizes the guests until Streiker himself shows up. In attempting to shoot Streiker, Loggia is killed. Then Adair learns that Fletcher left in order to take care of *her* business—to make contact with her estranged mother and stepfather, and to arrange a ballet audition for her. Further, the tasks he left for her were training to enable her to assist him in his work.

Adair then throws herself into ballet to the point that she neglects Fletcher. When she finally realigns her priorities and rejoins him, he tells her he has special business that he wants her to oversee. However, he is injured in a helicopter accident in the Hawaiian Islands and subsequently disappears. Adair then discovers that this special business is a child, Fletcher's son, Daniel.

The four-year-old is neglected, suspicious, and completely mute. Adair discovers that his mother filled him with fear of his father and supposedly died trying to run from Fletcher. As Adair grows to love Daniel, she works to win his trust enough to reconcile him to his father.

Meanwhile, she learns that Fletcher has many more enemies funded by the Warfield Group who are after Daniel as well. She finds out that her own father, Carl, is in their employ. But when Fletcher shows up again, she is able to convince Daniel to trust him, and they become a family.

When one of Fletcher's most valuable employees

is kidnaped by employees of the Warfield Group, Fletcher leads a rescue party after him. While he is gone, Daniel's mother, who had faked her death, shows up and tries to take Daniel away. But since he does not want to be separated from his father again, Adair fights her off. Fletcher returns with the rescued employee, and Daniel speaks for the first time.

---

1. Begun in *Streiker's Bride* and continued in *Streiker the Killdeer*.

≫ 1 ≪

A dair startled up at the train whistle's shrill hooting and looked out the window. The train she rode in, the Morning Sun, was passing through another small town, this one so sparsely lit at 2:00 a.m. that the fitful snow flurries obscured all but the closest, brightest streetlight.

Wiping the condensation of her breath from the window, Adair peered down the tracks ahead as far as she could. Where were they? With no visible signs, no telltale landmarks, it seemed as if this train had left the earth and landed again light-years away on some unknown planet.

Bony knees suddenly planted themselves in her lap, and Adair turned to redistribute the slight weight more comfortably on her legs. A soft little voice pleaded in her ear, "Mommy, I can't find Mr. Fuster and Daddy won't wake up."

"He's tired," Adair whispered. "Let me help you

find Mr. Fuster." She scooted four-year-old Daniel from her lap and knelt to the floor of the dark compartment, feeling under the seats. Mr. Fuster was the yellow bunny that had amassed some impressive mileage accompanying Daniel wherever he went. Right now friend Fuster had managed to hide himself very well in the small space of their private compartment. Adair paused and looked up as the train slowed to a stop with a groan and a sigh.

A light came on; Adair blinked at Fletcher lowering his hand from the overhead switch and slowly opening his eyes. Fletcher Streiker, the billionaire philanthropist whom the media dismissed as penniless since the sell-off of his corporation had begun several months ago, was in fact worth more now than he had ever been. Fletcher Streiker, the handsome Hawaiian-American whom "no one" had ever seen, was Adair's husband and Daniel's father, though the child was related by blood to neither of them. And Fletcher Streiker, the world traveler who owned a fleet of air, ground, and sea vehicles, was now taking his family anonymously by train to their midwinter destination.

"Daddy, you're squishing Mr. Fuster!" Daniel exclaimed, extracting the yellow lump of bunny from between Fletcher's hip and the side of his seat.

"Sorry. He crawled down there to get warm," Fletcher mumbled as Daniel wrapped Mr. Fuster up in his blankie and tucked them both safely under his chin. The blankie had no name other than "blankie."

There was a knock on the compartment door. "Beaconville, sir," called the porter from outside.

"Thank you," Fletcher called, glancing out the window as they got to their feet and stretched. Nothing was visible but the snow swirling close by outside. Daniel looked over, then leaned up close to the window to stare in wonder at the lacy snowflakes as they landed in delicate array on the outside of the glass. When he put his finger on the spot where one rested, it melted into a drop of water.

Adair pulled Daniel's hand away from the window to stuff it into the sleeve of his coat. "Is Harle meeting us here?" she asked Fletcher, referring to a favored employee. Although Daniel balked at the hood, she pulled it up and tied it under his chin.

"No, I left Harle in Dallas," Fletcher muttered tiredly as he shrugged on his own suede coat and held up hers.

"Well—you still haven't told me why we came here. I thought for sure you'd want to stay the winter in Honolulu," Adair said, meaning that *she* wanted to stay the winter in Hawaii. She loved Fletcher's house there, and they had just finished converting an upstairs room to a studio where Adair could begin teaching her newfound niece ballet.

As Adair buttoned her wool coat and tucked her blonde hair under her hat, Fletcher carefully placed his new black hat on his head and looked down his nose at her from under the low brim. "How do I look?" he asked.

She grinned. "Great. Really macho." The Stetson XXXX Beaver was Adair's Christmas present to him, as she had been appalled to discover that after all his years in Dallas, the billionaire had not one cowboy hat to his name.

Satisfied, he bent to take up their few suitcases. "You had better be wearing yours, then," he warned. He was referring to his Christmas present to her (part of it, anyway—his favorite part): a set of white silk lingerie. After seeing it on her, he went out the day after Christmas and bought up all the white silk he could

13

ROBIN HARDY

find, including slips, camisoles, and hosiery, until there
was enough for her to have a white Christmas in every
drawer in every house he owned.

"You bet I am," she smiled, kissing him under his
hat. "You were telling me why you decided to come
here?" she hinted.

"Um, I got a letter from somebody here who
needed help," he somewhat explained, hoisting their
suitcases.

"Oh," Adair replied. Despite the media's confidence
that he no longer had any money to give away, Fletcher
still received thousands of letters a week from hard-
luck cases who had heard of his generosity. Now he
chose one letter from among those thousands and
responded to it with a personal visit. Somehow, Adair
was not surprised. Fletcher had his own way of doing
things that usually confounded everybody at first, but
when she cooperated with him she found the experience worthwhile, to say the least.

When Daniel had tucked a securely bundled Mr.
Fuster into his nylon bag and zipped it up, they were
ready to go. Carrying their two leather suitcases,
Fletcher led the way down the narrow corridor and
turned off at the steps. As the porter opened the door
and hopped down to the platform, cold air shot through
the car. Fletcher stepped out and dropped the bags to
turn back for Daniel, waiting with arms outstretched.
Fletcher took his son in his arms while the porter
extended a hand to assist Adair out. Then Fletcher
dug in his pocket and handed the porter a folded bill.
The porter touched his hat and reboarded the train.
In just a few seconds it began to pull away from the
station, as the Streikers were the only ones disem-
barking at this place.

Adair watched the train depart, then turned to

14

the small building on their right. The station was dark, locked up tight. The only street visible past the tracks was empty of vehicles, as far as she could tell. A sports car parked near the brick station could have conceivably been hidden under the five-foot snowdrift. Texas born and bred, Adair had never seen such huge amounts of snow collected in one place. Neither had Daniel, who had not stopped shivering since coming off the train. He surveyed the bleak whiteness for only a moment before burying his face in his father's neck.

Adair quietly waited for Fletcher to lead. He glanced around in some dissatisfaction—someone who was supposed to be here was not. "Well," he mused, "I guess we walk."

His family accepted this without a murmur. For Daniel, clamped on his father's neck, it was a largely theoretical exercise anyway. Adair picked up the two suitcases and Fletcher reached over to take one, because Daniel was light enough to carry on one arm.

They trudged down from the platform on slippery, snow-crusted steps. "Careful," murmured Fletcher, reaching up an elbow for Adair to hold while descending the steps behind him. Snow was already collecting in the creases of his hat. They crossed over the tracks and stood in the middle of the street under the one working street lamp. Every building in view looked as lifeless as a mausoleum. Despite the protection of her wool coat, Adair was so chilled by the sight that her teeth began chattering.

Squinting against the snow flurries, Fletcher led up the street past several buildings before stopping at an office-supply store that had a light burning in an upper window. He banged loudly on the door, then stepped back to see if there was any activity behind the window. Adair thought she saw some movement, but no one came to the door, so they moved on.

"Here we go," Fletcher said in relief, spotting a pay phone on the street corner ahead. He hustled his family into the shelter of the booth, then squeezed in with them and started digging in his pockets for change. Adair came up with a quarter from her purse first.

Fletcher dropped in the quarter and waited, then hit the switch hook a few times. "Hello? Operator?" With creased brow he hung up, observing, "No dial tone." It didn't even return his quarter. Adair sighed in dismay, looking out at the snow flinging itself down to the street already clogged with the stuff. She began to fantasize about hot cocoa in front of a crackling fire.

The inside of the booth had begun to fog up when Fletcher pushed the door open, bringing in a fresh round of night cold. As tightly as Daniel was clinging to his father's neck, he wouldn't have dropped an inch had Fletcher let go of him.

They trudged back into the street. "It's a small town. There's gotta be a motel down around here some-where—probably near the interstate. I think it's that way," Fletcher nodded. They began briskly walking in that direction. His lips were already blue, and Adair remembered ironically how much he disliked cold weather. She was gratified that he was wearing the hat, at least. He hadn't thought to bring gloves.

"That must have been a real urgent letter," Adair mumbled, her jaw stiff with the cold. The complete question she had in mind was actually, *Why the heck did you drag us out here to Deadville or whatever it's called in the middle of the night while it's snowing and miserable, yet?*

"It's in my suitcase. You c-can look at it when we g-get settled," he said. Adair shook her head with a halfhearted smile—how could she get mad at him when he was as uncomfortable as anybody?—and trotted to keep as close as possible to him.

"There," Fletcher said triumphantly, and Adair looked up at the bright neon lights of the Best By Far Motel and Deli Bar, just past a church up ahead. Even Daniel risked raising his head from his father's shoulder to look at the beacon in the night.

They hurried to the motel's glass doors under the shelter of a large metal awning. Fletcher put his bag down and reached out a red hand to yank on the door handle, but it was bolted. Twenty feet away, encased in a protective glass booth, was the night manager. He was sound asleep in his chair.

Fletcher banged on the glass doors and shouted. Adair dropped her suitcase and pounded with the flats of her hands on the door. Daniel hollered with them, "Wake up, mister!" Oblivious, he slept on.

At this point Adair found the doorbell off to the side and rang it continuously. They watched with bated breath as the manager shifted, stretched, and then settled back to sleep in his chair.

"I don't believe this," Adair breathed, detaching her stiff finger from the doorbell. "Do you get the feeling we're not wanted here?"

Fletcher stepped back, evaluating the locked doors and the night manager nestled cozily in his heated office. Then he turned to look back down the street. The wind threatened to dislodge his hat, so he crammed it down harder on his head as he squinted through the snow. Relentless, the wind found what it could of Daniel's hair to whip out from under his hood.

"C'mon." With that short command, Fletcher picked up his suitcase and began stalking down the street the way they had come. Adair grabbed up her suitcase and followed. Daniel's light bag hung draped over Fletcher's shoulder, slapping him in the back as he walked.

Fletcher trotted up the white stone steps of the nearby church to try one handle of the massive oak doors. They were locked, of course, so he came back down and went around to the side of the church, illuminated by the motel's neon lights. It was not a very big building.

Stopping at a dark side door surrounded by frozen ivy, Fletcher tried that handle. He did not seem surprised to find this one locked as well, for he put Daniel down, took a step back and kicked the door in with a resounding bang that dislodged a shower of snow from the roof. "Yea!" Daniel cheered, and Adair looked around as if expecting to get caught.

"Here we go," Fletcher said in satisfaction, leading them inside and shutting the splintered door. It was very dark and cold inside, so Adair just held Daniel still while Fletcher groped for a light switch.

He found one and clicked it on. Adair shaded her eyes, then squinted around at the desk, filing cabinets, and bulletin board in the small church office. Fletcher went straight to a thermostat and turned it on. Hearing the grumbling of a furnace firing up, Adair sighed.

"Now let's find a place to bed down for a few hours," Fletcher proposed. Adair, holding Daniel's hand, peeked into the minister's study off the outer office. It was so small that one desk, two chairs, and a floor lamp filled it entirely. There was no room for anyone larger than a four-year-old to lie down.

They went down the hall, clicking on lights as they came upon switches, and looked into a kitchen area with cold linoleum flooring. Daniel shivered. On down the hall were two supply closets and then the sanctuary, which could probably seat seventy-five if they were all friendly toward each other. Fletcher turned up the chandeliers to fully illumine it.

It was a beautiful room built of stone and timber, with four large stained-glass windows set in the walls—two toward the front near the dais with its podium, and two in the back near the double oak doors. The front of the small auditorium was closer to the interior of the building, and the back was closer to the street, as is customary. One anomaly Adair did not notice right away was that there was no foyer. Anyone entering the doors would find himself directly among the pews. The flashing neon lights next door gave a surreal appearance to the left rear window, farthest away from the podium, and alternately colored the interior stonework red and blue. Plush carpet covered the floor beneath stately oak pews.

When Daniel felt the warm air coming from a floor vent near the stone wall, he sat down right next to it and retrieved bunny and blankie from his nylon bag. Tucking Mr. Fuster under his arm, he twisted a corner of the blankie to a point, stuffed it in his mouth, lay down, and shut his eyes.

Adair looked up at Fletcher with a wry smile. "Daniel has decided we'll sleep here," she whispered.

Fletcher kissed her on the temple. "Then you wait with him while I see if I can find any blankets," he said. None of them had unbuttoned their coats yet. She nodded and sat, tucking her coat around her knees. On his way out, he dimmed the sanctuary lights to a comfortable low glow.

While Fletcher was gone Adair studied the left rear window, being the only one lit well enough to see in detail. It depicted Jesus standing at the door and knocking. This was the familiar portrayal of Jesus

19

from her childhood, with flowing brown hair, Anglo features, and creamy white robe. The window was a beautiful piece of art, painstakingly crafted, but it left her vaguely dissatisfied. What was wrong with it?

It made her think of her first ballet lessons, when she was four. Step and point, turn and point, over and over—they were cruelly boring. But since her mother had forced her to stay with it, the discipline of those early steps had opened up a marvelous world of beauty and expression. But what if, twenty years later, she still danced ballet as she had danced it at four?

She thought of learning to read at six, and the insipid text of those early books: "See the dog. See the dog run. The dog can run fast. Can you run fast, too?" Nothing in those books had excited her to read, but the teachers who forced her to master them and go on had opened up worlds of enlightenment to her. But what if, eighteen years later, she still read as she did at six?

Then she thought about her conceptions of God as her heavenly Father. With a child's reasoning, she had long ago decided that as her father, Carl, was short-tempered, critical, and largely unavailable, then God must be too, only more so. Was this immature assessment of Him valid? Tonight was the first time this question had crossed her mind.

So that must be the problem with the window. These bland pictures of Jesus were fine for children, but adults who clung to them found them insufficient for adult-sized frames. No prima ballerina performed "Step and Point" at the Met, and no CEO carried *See the Dog* into board meetings. So grownups—like herself—who refused to grow past a child's understanding of God were asking for disappointment at the most crucial times of their lives. What worlds would open up to someone who moved on to a more realistic picture?

"I'm making too much out of a window," Adair sighed, shaking her hair down from the wool hat. Then she looked up expectantly as Fletcher came back in.

He sat beside her, placing a carton, box, and plastic glasses on the floor. "I couldn't find any blankets, but here's some grape juice and crackers. Want some?" he whispered.

"I do!" Daniel said suddenly, sitting up. Chuckling, Fletcher poured him a half glass as Daniel raided the cracker box.

Adair hesitated. "Should we drink this?"

"I don't think it's poisoned or anything," Fletcher said mildly, pouring a second glass.

"No, I mean, it's probably for Communion," Adair whispered.

"I'll pay for it, and the door," he assured her.

"But wouldn't it be—disrespectful?" she balked as he handed her the glass.

Fletcher glanced at Daniel draining his cup and presenting it for a refill. "It's just grape juice, Adair. Here, will this make you feel better?" Fletcher asked, lifting his cup and looking to the ceiling, "God, thanks for allowing three stranded travelers the shelter of Your house and the provision of Your refrigerator on one hell of a night. Amen."

"Amen!" agreed Daniel, coated in cracker crumbs, and Adair stifled a laugh as she took the cup Fletcher offered.

When they had finished their snack, Fletcher returned the leftovers to the kitchen. By then the vents had warmed them enough so they could take off their coats. Daniel lay down again and Adair put his coat over him for a comforter, kissing him good night. He was asleep before his dad even got back.

Lying down beside Adair, Fletcher slipped a hand under her sweater to feel the silk camisole. Then he sighed and closed his eyes.

✳

Hours later, Adair woke from a leaden rest to see her forearm painted purple and gold by the morning sun shining in through the window above her. Stretching on the carpet, she looked up at the window. Jesus, ablaze with light, now looked to be crashing down the door at which He stood. "That's more like it," she murmured, rubbing a pinched nerve in her neck.

Fletcher was sitting up, tinkering with his watch. "With the time change, that puts us at eight-thirty," he muttered, then looked over and smiled. "Good morning."

"Um-hmm," she replied, leaning into his shoulder. With his wrinkled shirttail sticking out from under his sweater and his black hair mussed over his forehead, he reminded her of a third-grader who slept in his clothes to save time in the morning. But this boy's tanned face sported the scruffy start of a beard and serious eyes that were slightly swollen from the dry heat. Adair didn't even want to think about how she looked after sleeping in her clothes. At least she had learned not to wear as much makeup that would get smeared all over her face. With Fletcher always taking off at a moment's notice, she never had time to apply it.

He kissed her tangled hair and they both regarded Daniel, still asleep, curled up in a tight ball next to the floor vent. Adair mused, "I still can't get over how much he looks like you. It's almost enough to make me suspicious that you might be his father after all," she added wickedly.

Rather than foam with righteous indignation, Fletcher merely raised a brow as he replaced the watch on his arm. "You know, somebody was telling me the other day how much you and I look alike."

"You and I!" Adair exclaimed.

"Yep. How much you were getting to look like me," he casually elaborated.

"That's ridiculous!" Adair laughed. "You're a man and I'm a woman! You're dark and I'm blonde. And I would punch out anybody who said my feet looked like yours!"

"Not in that way. You're talking about superficialities. But what you really notice about somebody's appearance is facial expression, attitude, outlook—those things that come from inside you," he said. He sat on his knees to lift the sleeping boy to his shoulder. "Face it, people who spend a lot of time together better have the basics in common, right?" He got to his feet with Daniel, smiling lightly.

Gathering up an empty carton and used glasses, she conceded, "Maybe. But maybe that means you're getting to look like me."

"I hate to be the one to break this to you," he said without remorse as he took up a suitcase, "but you're the one who's changed the most. I can remember a time when you would've thrown a hissy fit about arriving at a strange town in the middle of the night without someone to usher you straight to comfortable quarters."

Adair winced, "Can we talk about something else?" and Fletcher laughed. Daniel raised his head, rubbing his eyes.

They availed themselves of the lavatory off the minister's study and bundled up in their coats. In the outer office, Fletcher paused to turn off the heater and dig in his pocket. He left enough cash on the desk to pay for the door, the refreshments, and a gym, if the church fathers so desired.

They stepped out into the crisp morning. The sunlight that had illumined her window was now obscured by low, heavy clouds shedding random snowflakes. Reflecting back to his comment, Adair admitted, "I *was* wondering why you didn't have someone drive us, or at least meet us here."

"The roads around here were totally impassable yesterday," Fletcher said. "I told the woman who wrote me that we were coming, and asked her to meet our train. I thought she should have an opportunity to help answer her own request."

"She blew it," Adair noted sternly.

"She'll have another chance," Fletcher said. With Daniel on his arm again, they trudged in the general area of the sidewalk through the packed drifts to the Best By Far Motel.

The glass doors under the metal awning were still locked, but the day manager responded promptly to the ring of the doorbell. "Well, good morning!" he said in surprise as he opened the doors. "I sure wasn't expectin' anybody till this weekend, at least. Where you folks from?"

"Dallas," Fletcher said. "We'd like a room with two double beds, please," he said, dropping a suitcase and repositioning Daniel to sign in.

"Dallas, eh? Sure, uh, Mr. Streiker," the manager said pleasantly, noting the sign-in form. He showed no recognition of the name. Adair was a little surprised that Fletcher would sign his own name, as he rarely divulged his identity when he traveled. But he did not lie, either, and Adair guessed so few people in this little town had heard of him that he felt it safe to call himself who he was.

Fletcher was handed a key and directed down the corridor. "Good room, too—right next to the ice machine," the manager noted.

"Um-hmm," Fletcher murmured absently, shifting his sleepy son.

Down the hall and next to the ice machine, Fletcher unlocked the door of their room and opened it. It was a boxy little room barely big enough for the two beds, a dresser, and a television set securely bolted down. They filed in and dropped their suitcases on the floor, all of them eyeing the beds with some resentment that they weren't accessible last night.

While Adair bathed Daniel, Fletcher got them some breakfast from the deli bar. Shortly after Daniel was freshly dressed, he was sitting on the edge of one bed with a Styrofoam plate of ham and potato salad, swinging his legs and watching cartoons.

When Adair came out of the shower, Fletcher was hanging up the phone. "Keeping in touch, though the surcharges for long-distance calls from here are liable to hit the moon," he noted.

"Spendthrift," Adair chided, toweling her hair.

"You complaining?" he wondered.

"Not me," she said hastily. "How's the sell-off going?"

"Chuck said everything's well in hand," Fletcher said, moving to the television to lower the volume of space blasters, "except. . . ."

"Except what?" Adair asked anxiously.

"Your dad, Carl, gave Reggie the slip again, running blind and scared. He won't talk to any of my people, and I'm afraid he's going to get himself hurt shooting off like that," Fletcher said heavily.

"Like Sandra did," Adair mused. This was Daniel's mother, who had tried everything short of murder to keep him away from Fletcher.

"Yeah, like Sandra. I was hoping Carl would be more disposed to listen to me, but now I have to weigh whether it's doing more harm than good to keep after him," Fletcher thought out loud. Adair did not voice an opinion, so he decided, "I'll let him chill for a while before I try again." She smiled. Fletcher had a tenacity that few people could comprehend. He glanced over to appraise the silk underwear she took out of her suitcase, then nodded in approval.

On his way back to the bathroom, Fletcher dropped a small envelope in her lap. "Have a look. It's from the woman who lives here." He paused. "Unless . . . you'd rather join me in the shower," he invited, unbuttoning his shirt.

Daniel wiped cookie crumbs from his mouth with his sleeve and scrambled down from the bed. "I'll play in the shower with you, Daddy!"

"You just sit there and watch 'Rowdy Rangers'," Fletcher instructed with mock peevishness, but his glance toward Adair was somewhat wistful. Daniel obediently climbed back onto the bed.

Adair winked at her husband, and he pulled out shaving gear in resignation. Then she opened up the letter. With interest, she read:

Dear Mr. Streiker,

My name is Lilith Crandall. I've heard so much about you, and I thought that if anybody could help us here in Beaconville, you could. There's no reason why you should from your point of view. What I mean is, we don't have much to offer you. But I was thinking that if you could meet some of our people and see what we're about, then you might see your way clear to give us a hand.

Thank you,
Lilith Crandall

Adair held the letter blankly while Fletcher shaved and showered. When he turned off the water and reached for a towel, she went to the door of the tiny bathroom to hand him one. "Is this a joke?" she asked.

"What, me taking a cold shower? I'm not laughing," he said, vigorously rubbing down.

Adair glanced at his physique and smiled. "No. This letter," she clarified.

Fletcher looked over his shoulder as he hung up the towel. "What makes you say that?"

"Well, this . . . it's so vague. She doesn't even say what she wants you to do. What made you drop everything to respond in person to this?" she wondered.

Shaking out underwear, Fletcher said, "Actually, it's more what she didn't say. She didn't ask for money. She didn't say *me* or *I*, but *we* and *us*. She couldn't put a finger on what was troubling her, but I happen to know that the Warfield Group has completely overrun this area."

Adair tensed at the mention of this name. This was a well-heeled, widespread organization, the main interest of which seemed to be in discrediting Fletcher. "So I just thought we'd come see what we could do," he said from under a sweater. Pulling it on over his head, he regarded her with one of his canny smiles.

"I see," she murmured, and she did. Knowing that the town was under siege by his enemies, Fletcher had been looking for an excuse to come do something about

27

it. And Lilith's plea, vague and rambling as it was, provided that open door.

As soon as Fletcher was dressed they started from the room. Eyeing bunny and blankie clinging stubbornly to Daniel, Adair observed, "It might be fun to play in the snow, only Mr. Fuster doesn't like the cold. And poor blankie would get all wet and droopy. Don't you think they'd rather wait for you in the nice warm room?" she coaxed, gently disengaging them from the little fingers.

"If Mr. Fuster tries to burrow down in this snow, we won't find him again until next spring," Fletcher solemnly added. So Daniel was persuaded to leave his companions behind in the safety of the motel room.

Then Fletcher escorted his family out to the drab motel lobby and paid the day manager to call a cab for them—the one cab in the whole city operating today, the manager was quick to point out. When it arrived, Fletcher gave the cabbie the return address from Lilith's letter and they climbed in. Adair did not see much scenery on the way, being too preoccupied with dissuading Daniel from investigating the trash strewn about the floorboard of the cab, but the ride was a short one.

They pulled up to a two-story white frame house with black shutters sitting behind a wooden fence. Getting out, Fletcher handed the driver just enough to cover the fare rather than one of his usual Ben Franklins. The cabbie eyed the paltry amount and sneered, "Have a nice day, pal." Fletcher did not respond.

As the cab skidded away from the curb, scattering snow, Fletcher led through the gate in the fence (frozen half-open) and they went up the walk to the front door. It was painted black, protected by a screen door, which should have long ago been replaced with a storm door.

Fletcher rang the doorbell and stepped back.

A moment later the door slowly opened. A broad, fortyish woman in a bulky sweater and stretch pants looked apprehensively at the family on her front porch. "I'm looking for Lilith Crandall," Fletcher said.

"That's me," she replied in a faint voice.

"Lilith, I'm Fletcher Streiker," he said, and she gazed at him in utter disbelief.

❊ 2 ❊

"**Y**ou wrote me, asking for help," Fletcher reminded a stricken Lilith. "I wrote you back and told you I'd be coming on last night's train."

"I. . . ." She opened her mouth helplessly. "Did you come?"

"Yes," he said without sarcasm, "and I brought my family. This is my wife, Adair, and my son, Daniel. Uh, can we come in?" They were still standing out in the cold.

"Well, yes, of course, come on in." Lilith turned, shooing a curious, longhaired cat out from underfoot. "Cody! Come get your junk! Oh—the house is just a mess. I can't believe it. I got your letter, but everybody said it was a joke. I can't believe you actually came." She put a fretful hand to the curlers in her hair as she showed them into a cozy, cluttered den with a large fireplace that was in use.

31

Daniel was barely out of his coat before dropping to his knees to pursue the beautiful sandy Persian under the coffee table. Adair and Fletcher shrugged out of their coats and held them uncertainly a moment. Since Lilith was too distracted clearing away dirty dishes to offer to hang them somewhere, they just draped them across the back of a nubby brown couch. Fletcher took off his hat and placed it upside down on the dusty end table next to the couch.

A skinny teenager shuffled into the room and carelessly swept up a pair of high-tops without laces, glancing idly at the strangers. Coming from the kitchen, Lilith said, "This is my son Cody. They're out of school today because of the snow. Cody, this is Mr. Streiker and his family!" She meanwhile waved at them to sit down.

"Right. And I'm Tupac Shakur. Pleased ta meet ya," Cody snorted. At fifteen, he had erratically cut brown hair and a war on with acne.

"Cody!" Lilith exclaimed in embarrassment. Then she hesitantly asked Fletcher, "You . . . wouldn't have any identification on you, would you?"

"No. Just the letter you sent me," Fletcher said. Taking it from his back pocket, he tossed it on the coffee table in front of them as he and Adair sat on the couch. She eyed Daniel crawling on the floor under the table, but decided it would create more of a disturbance to get him out than leave him be. The cat had skittered to safety elsewhere.

"That's the letter," Lilith admitted dubiously. Cody looked back at her with contempt as he collected a sweater and coat, then dumped the whole armload of apparel in the next room.

"So tell me what you wanted me to do for you," Fletcher said, resting his elbows on his knees.

"Well, I . . . just can't think right now," Lilith stammered. Cody came back to watch skeptically, leaning on the door-frame between the den and television room.

"In your letter, you implied I'd be more disposed to help you if I saw your town. What did you want to show me?" Fletcher asked.

Lilith began slowly, then gathered steam: "Well, there's so many good folks here—so many people who'd just give you the shirt off their backs, if you needed it, but it seems like all the sudden we've been hit with one thing or another. First it was the plant closing, and then that fire that took out most of Seventh Street—"

"God, Mom!" Cody uttered in disgust, looking away.

Fletcher looked at him attentively. "Excuse me—are you praying?"

"Huh? No," Cody said with derision.

"You said God, so I thought you must be praying," Fletcher said.

"Wrongo," Cody said with curled lip.

"If you didn't mean it as a prayer, then what did you mean?" Fletcher asked, appearing genuinely curious.

"It is an expression of disgust that my mother is stupid enough to sit here and talk with an obvious con as if he was really Fletcher Streiker," Cody said pretentiously.

"Oh," Fletcher said, seriously trying not to smile.

Daniel looked out sternly from under the coffee table and demanded, "What're you callin' my daddy?"

"Shh, Daniel," Adair whispered.

"If I were God," Fletcher observed, "I think I'd get ticked off at somebody who used my name as an expression of disgust. Suppose I went around saying, 'Oh, Cody!' every time I stepped in a pile of dog poop?"

"Why don't you just stuff it?" Cody asked irately.

"Cody Crandall, I've heard enough of you! This man

is our guest and you can be cordial or just go to your room!" Lilith ordered. Adair noticed she didn't admit that Fletcher was who he said he was.

"That's okay, Lilith; he's just honing his debating skills. Second place citywide—that's pretty good. You might have taken first had you chosen a more original topic to debate than the death penalty," Fletcher said easily.

Everybody grew still and Adair regarded Fletcher with raised brow. Not that she was surprised; now she knew what he had stayed up so late reading right before they left.

"How did you know about that?" Cody asked faintly.

"I research everybody I initiate personal contact with," Fletcher replied. "Ask my wife."

"Thoroughly," Adair agreed wryly. "Before he proposed to me, he knew everything about me but my shoe size."

"Seven and a half," he promptly replied, turning.

"I was just making a point," she muttered, embarrassed.

"Then—you know all about me?" Lilith asked timidly.

"I know a lot," Fletcher admitted.

"Tell me about Maynard, then," Cody challenged.

"Cody!" Lilith exclaimed, coloring.

"Maynard Crandall is your dad. You haven't seen him in thirteen years, and Lilith divorced him *in absentia* about ten years ago. I know where he is, if you're interested," Fletcher related.

Lilith and Cody looked stunned. "You ain't for real!" Cody sputtered.

"It'd be easy enough to find out," Fletcher said, digging in his pockets. "Drat. Forgot the phone number," he muttered, emptying one pocket of a wad of hundred-dollar bills. Lilith drew a quick breath and Cody dropped his jaw at the sight. "Anyway, I know he's staying at the Chisholm Motel in Bellwright. He hasn't contacted you because he's afraid of being charged with desertion," Fletcher said.

"How do you know that?" Cody asked between shallow breaths.

"I talked to him," Fletcher said, glancing up as he continued to rummage through his clothes. "Adair, did you see where I might've laid a yellow envelope?"

"Was it on the kitchen table at home?" she asked. Daniel slid out from under the table to gather several errant cat's-eyes from the floor.

"Probably. Rats. Well, the upshot is, he's willing to talk to you if he's sure you won't press charges. That's how he put it, but I think what he's really after is your forgiveness," Fletcher told them, looking straight at Lilith.

Cody stood motionless, staring off, but Lilith began yanking curlers from her head and vigorously fluffing the short brown curls. "Ten years without one word, one red cent to help raise his son, and *he's* willing to talk to us! Since we've been getting by without him all this time, I think we can do without Mr. Crandall just fine now, thank you very much!"

But Cody's face had settled into an expression of hostile intent that Adair recognized, remembering that first evening she had sat in her apartment and opened Fletcher's file folder. The hope stirred by his interest was too painful to harbor—better dash it to pieces quickly before it could take root and grow. So when Cody suddenly left the doorway, Adair knew he was heading for a telephone.

They heard him in the kitchen saying, "Gimme the

number for the Chisholm Motel in Bellwright."

"Cody!" Lilith shouted toward the kitchen. But she appeared cemented to her chair, unable to do anything further to stop him.

"Okay," he said, muffled, then a few moments later they heard, "Yeah, gimme Maynard Crandall's room. . . . No? Where is he? Yeah." Another short interval passed and he said, "Is Maynard Crandall there? Can I talk to him?"

When he spoke again his voice was so low they could barely hear him. "Maynard? This Maynard? This is Cody . . . your son Cody. Yeah! How're ya doin', Dad?"

He began talking in a pent-up rush, assuring his father repeatedly that they wouldn't have him arrested and didn't want money, they only wanted to see him. Lilith listened to Cody's end of the conversation with a white face and tight lips.

"Yeah, the snow's real bad here, too. The buses couldn't run and they closed school today. But when it clears up, d'you think you can get on out? We live at Twelve Seventy-five Maple. Yeah, still in Beaconville. . . . Hey, did a Fletcher Streiker call you? Yeah? Yeah, he's sittin' right here in our front room," Cody said.

"That's long-distance, Cody Crandall!" His mother shouted a desperate reminder.

"Uh, listen, Dad, I gotta hang up. But you come on out when the roads clear, okay? Mom's a great cook and we'll feed you some of her lemon-barbecue chicken. Okay? Cool. 'Bye, Dad."

A moment later Cody returned to the front room, unsure of what all the others might have overheard. "I got hold of Maynard at the Texaco where he works. He said somebody calling himself Fletcher Streiker called him—not that he believed you or anything," Cody hastened to add. "And it's not like I believe you either."

"It's a moot point to say you don't believe me when you called him anyway," Fletcher noted. It took a few seconds for Cody to apprehend that.

Lilith stirred. "Well, seeing as you *are* here [and she looked not so sure about it] I suppose what we need to do is take you around for a tour. We can't go far—I can't even get the car out of the garage—but it's a short walk downtown and I guess it'll be enough to show you what we're like."

"That's fine," Fletcher said, standing.

Daniel stood as well, imitating Fletcher's posture and stance. "I havta go to the potty," he announced.

Lilith cracked a smile. "Down the hall, to your left."

"Let me help you, Daniel," Adair said, taking his hand. He protested, being quite capable of going alone, but Adair led him down the hall, into the bathroom, and shut the door. She then emptied his pockets of all the marbles he had collected from the floor. Daniel whined severely, but she stood firm: "These aren't ours to take. Go potty now."

"Daddy will pay for them," he said sullenly, pulling down his jeans.

"Daddy may not want to," Adair overruled.

"But *I* want them," Daniel fussed.

"You can't have everything you want," Adair said impatiently.

"Why not? You told Daddy you have everything you want," he said accusingly.

Adair laughed in surprise. "Why—that's true. But that's because I don't want everything I see. Now that I could buy anything, I realize most of it's just junk," she reflected.

"Marbles is not junk," he said stubbornly, stooping to raise his pants again.

"Daniel," she said, kneeling before him to help him

zip his jeans, "let me tell you a little story. This is about a boy who loved marbles. One day he went to Marbletown, where marbles are just lying around all over, in the streets, everywhere. He picked up all the marbles he could find and stuffed his pockets full of them, until he weighed two hundred pounds with all the marbles. Then he was walking along the sidewalk when he slipped on some loose marbles and fell into six feet of snow. With all those marbles weighing him down, he fell through all six feet of snow and nobody could find him until six months later when the snow began to thaw, and by then he was frozen hard as a marble."

Daniel eyed her suspiciously. "You're just making that up."

"Yes, I am. But you still can't take the marbles," she said. Grudgingly, he left them on the bathroom counter without further argument.

They came back out to the front room where Fletcher was waiting with their coats. As he slipped Adair's over her arms, she glanced back at the sly anticipation in his face. "We're moving right along," he noted quietly. This was the first inkling Adair had that he already knew what he was going to do here. Thinking back, she realized she should have known all along that he would have come with a well-formulated plan. He began to say more, but Lilith and Cody appeared in the foyer, dressed to go out. Cody had merely thrown a hooded sweatshirt over his flannel shirt, but Lilith had put on a heavy coat and combed out her hair before pushing it all under a stocking cap.

"Thought I'd just come watch," Cody said aloofly. Fletcher smiled, flipping his hat deftly before plopping it on his head. Cody was caught briefly eyeing him in admiration, and even Adair wondered who taught Fletcher how a Texan handles his hat.

The cold hit them like a brick when they walked out of the warm house. The sun, a pale circle behind seamless clouds, gave just enough light to make the icicles on the lamppost glitter. At some point snow had been bulldozed off this narrow street only to uncover the layer of ice beneath it. Stepping carefully along the slippery sidewalk clutching Daniel's hand, Adair glanced up at two of Lilith's young neighbors ice-skating down the street.

The houses along this heavily treed street and the next were all two-story, wood-frame structures built in a similar style about fifty years ago. The first impression they gave was that of a charming throwback to a bygone era. Had Adair a chance to look closer, she would have seen the peeling paint, broken windows, rotting wood, and cracked foundations that sucked enough charm from the nostalgia for several owners to abandon them. Ironically, the abandoned houses didn't look much worse than the occupied ones.

Walking another block brought them to a strip shopping center along part of the main drag. Continual puffs of steam trailed Lilith as she talked busily to Fletcher, pointing out this and that, but Adair stopped listening after five minutes of discourse on the new sign ordinance. Last month's Christmas decorations drooped from street signs and corner lights. What with the demands of clearing roadways on a three-person city crew, no one had yet had the opportunity to take down old candy canes.

Daniel, snow encrusted up to his knees, looked up and said, "Mommy, they ain't had Christmas yet."

"'Ain't'?" Adair blinked, as that was the first time she'd heard him use this word.

"It's come and gone, like everything else here," Cody said tiredly. "Come and gone, and nothing changes."

"This here's the jewelry store, and the five-and-dime—it's actually Mulroney's but nobody calls it that; it's the five-and-dime. Next to that is the Country Attic Gift Shop," Lilith pointed out. Fletcher nodded, his silent breath steaming in the cold air. The stalwart proprietors had opened their shops, but there were no customers so far this morning.

Adair drew up close to Fletcher for warmth as he paused in front of the Delightfully Yours Jewelry Store. A small sign in the corner of the window advertised, "A locally owned and operated franchise." "Delightfully Yours is a subsidiary of the Warfield Group," Fletcher whispered to her. With flushed cheeks, he cupped his bare hands over his mouth and breathed on them, thinking.

Then he reached out and opened the door. A little bell jangled as they entered the comparative warmth of the shop, and the owner came up eagerly to greet them. She was a fashionably slender woman with heavy makeup and lots of teeth. "Lilith! How are you?" she said with an inquisitive glance at her guests. Another woman who had been loitering over the display cases looked up.

"Just real good, Daynell. This is Mr. Fletcher Streiker and his family, who I wrote, remember?" Lilith said, evidently deciding to throw her weight behind his claim after all. "This is Daynell Rodgers. She and Powell—her husband—design the prettiest pieces you ever saw."

"Nice shop," Fletcher observed in what Adair sensed was an opening move.

"We have a special of thirty percent off all gemstones," Daynell offered.

"Really," he murmured, glancing in the showcases. "How's business with Delightfully Yours?"

40

"Just—delightful!" Daynell laughed.

Fletcher continued perusing the cases. "Is that right? Then they've helped you a lot?"

Daynell opened her mouth to respond with a light-hearted affirmative, but Fletcher looked her in the eye and she paused. Not many people demanded the truth in superficial conversations. "Well," she faltered, "to be honest, they're so big, and I'm such a little operation—why should they bother with me? I'm lucky they give me anything at all. Actually, I . . . they're draining the life out of me. There are all sorts of hidden fees, and they haven't provided hardly anything they promised. I never hear from them except if I'm late with a payment I didn't even know about, and then I get a form letter from their legal department. I'm just at the end of my rope," she said quietly, blinking. The other woman, who had not been introduced, came over to put her arm around Daynell.

"Sounds like you have ample reason to break the franchise agreement," Fletcher said. Adair noted the seamless move from opening to proposition. Daniel was fidgeting impatiently, so Fletcher picked him up and held him. He laid his head on his daddy's shoulder, tracing patterns with his fingers on the suede coat.

"I don't know how. I can't afford a lawyer," Daynell admitted despondently. Proposition meets resistance, Adair noted.

Smiling, Fletcher turned from the counter to browse leisurely through the rest of the store, giving Daynell time to get her hopes up. "Nice shop," he repeated. "Jewelry has a nice high markup and investment value. Tell you what," he offered, turning back to Daynell. "If you want to get out from under Delightfully Yours, I'll help you. I'll provide legal expertise and financing for half of what you're paying them."

41

"You would?" gasped Daynell. Resistance is zapped. Adair watched Fletcher for his follow-through, as did the nameless woman.

"Yep." He returned to the counter and picked up a notepad and pen with his free hand. "This is the number of Yvonne Fay, my assistant in Dallas. Tell her what I told you, and she'll work up a new agreement between you and me. Deal?"

"Why—why—" Daynell was so astonished she could hardly speak, but Fletcher took that for assent and turned to the door. Adair shook her head in admiration, thinking, *He's good.*

As a finishing touch, he added, "Oh, and pick out something nice for Lilith. Tell Yvonne the price when you call her so she can include it in the draft."

"Mr. Streiker!" Lilith exclaimed in pleasant surprise.

"Cody, you come with us," Fletcher instructed as he swung open the door.

"Uh—sure." Surprised to be included, Cody agreed without any of the sarcasm he had used earlier.

"Mr. Streiker." The unknown woman came forward, and Fletcher paused at the door to look at her for the first time. With her smooth pageboy, tasteful makeup, and impeccable wool suit, she appeared out of place in Beaconville. "My name is Edwina Moos," she introduced herself, offering her hand. Fletcher released the door to shake her hand without replying. Lilith rolled her eyes behind Edwina's back.

"Might I assume that, as a person of influence, you have an interest in art?" Edwina asked stiffly, implying that he should.

"I don't purchase much, but I commission a lot," Fletcher replied.

"Then you really should come look at my gallery. I have many interesting, avant-garde pieces—nothing

42

commercial, you understand. Only for the connoisseur," she said haughtily.

Fletcher hesitated. Adair read his interest level at zero, but he said, "I'll come look." Whereupon Ms. Moos smugly escorted him next door to the Edwina Moos Art Gallery—a shop Lilith had neglected to point out.

As Ms. Moos unlocked the door of her store, she glanced back at Cody trailing the Streikers. "I don't allow children in my gallery," she said coldly, and Cody glared back at her.

"Then I'll have to pass," Fletcher said, turning away with Daniel on his shoulder.

She caught his arm. "I'll make an exception today." To Cody, she said sternly, "Please do keep your distance from the pieces. They're very valuable," but that did not stop him from gloating.

"Maybe," Fletcher grunted as they entered the cold gallery. Edwina went to check the thermostat, but did not touch it.

"It's really frosty in here," Cody observed, bouncing in his sweatshirt.

"Heat is terribly destructive to art," Edwina replied condescendingly, then turned to Fletcher to introduce the works she had available.

He glanced around at the largely modern, wholly abstract designs mounted around the room. "Okay, I've seen enough," he said, turning toward the door.

She caught his arm again. "Wait! I haven't begun to tell you about the artists I represent."

"Ms. Moos, I'm not interested in anything here," he said plainly.

"I see. You must be a follower of realism, then," she said, eyes half-closed in disdain.

"The style is irrelevant. I commission works from all across the spectrum. It is the actuating spirit behind the piece that interests me," he said.

"Really," she said. "How intriguing. May I ask how you ascertain that?"

"It's easy. I get to know all the artists I work with, and they me. I let them know exactly what I expect of them—their job is to communicate the truth as they have experienced it. How successful they are depends on how accurately they reproduce in their particular medium the vision I give them," Fletcher said.

Edwina stared at him with her lips twisted in almost a sneer. "Reproducing *your* vision—I'm afraid it sounds rather oppressive, for an artist."

Fletcher smiled. "Actually, they tell me they feel like pioneers. Doing it my way enables them to convey something understandable in completely new ways. Also, they don't have to worry about producing something strictly 'commercial,' mass-market. Since I'm the one paying them, they can express whatever is on their hearts and never worry about starving. That's what I consider avant-garde. Now, I'll be willing to invest in your gallery if you'll be willing to introduce your artists to me."

"*My* artists have no interest in becoming robots on your little assembly line," Edwina replied, folding her skeletal hands. From this comment, Adair gleaned that she had not understood anything he had said.

Fletcher nodded. "The offer stands for the next three days." He opened the door and they left. Cody kept looking at him as if he wanted to say something, but gave up and kept quiet.

They went to the five-and-dime store on the other side of the jewelry shop. "Who owns this?" Fletcher asked Cody.

"I dunno—somebody out of town. Jerry Hayworth's the manager," Cody offered, holding the door for the group.

This store was reminiscent of the fifties in everything from the layout and shelf displays to the cheap merchandise that children loved. Daniel promptly wriggled from Fletcher's arms to drop on his knees and examine a row of plastic gadgets. "Hey, Jerry!" called Cody, and a gruff fellow in rumpled shirt and glasses straightened from a lower shelf he was restocking.

"Jerry, this is the billionaire that my mom wrote to. He just bought Daynell's store," Cody informed him importantly.

"'S that right?" Hayworth muttered, studying Fletcher over his bifocals.

"Yeah, and he was askin' who owns this place," Cody added.

"I don't see why you'd be interested in that," Jerry said mildly. His cool manner relayed the underlying message, *None of your business. Big billionaire thinks he can traipse into town and buy up everything he sees. Harumph!*

"I'm not, really," Fletcher shrugged. "The jewelry store had some merit, but this. . . ." He eyed boxes of pencil erasers with a touch of humorous disdain, and Adair witnessed another smooth opening, custom-tailored.

Jerry came out from behind the counter to defend his operation. "I'll have you know that we've had the highest gross of any retail outlet in Beaconville for four of the last five months."

"Really?" Fletcher said, looking surprised.

"That's right. And the way I see it, that's because the owner leaves me alone and lets me run it just the way I want. No way would I want to have that changed," Jerry declared, as though the decision to sell were up to him.

"An individual owns it?" Fletcher asked skeptically,

wandering down a solid aisle of ponytail holders, hair clips, and curlers.

"JB McConklin of Atlanta, Georgia, who's wealthier than you'll ever be," Jerry snorted, following him closely.

Fletcher turned. "JB died last week. His estate's in probate, which means there's no telling who'll own you shortly." Jerry's face went slack, and he stood there with arms hanging.

Daniel came up and tugged on his father's hand. "Daddy, will you buy me this?" he asked, holding up a macho plastic figure wearing ammo belts, tight pants, and a blonde ponytail. "It's Beef Jerky, from 'Rowdy Rangers.'"

Fletcher regarded the action figure with a pained expression. "The cartoon you were watching this morning, huh? Daniel, I don't think you'll be happy with that for very long."

Daniel screwed up his little face. "But I want it. Please get it for me, Daddy. Please, please, please." He knew better than to raise his voice, but he did beg with all the earnestness of a needy child.

While the manager watched silently, Fletcher sighed, then began pulling bills from his pocket. "Adair, do you have a small bill? I don't think Mr. Hayworth can change a hundred this early in the day."

"Sure," Adair murmured, swinging her purse from her shoulder onto the counter. Daniel happily presented for purchase the scowling figure, complete with miniature AK-47.

Jerry went to the cash register to ring up the sale. At that time Lilith came in the door with a bang. "Mr. Streiker!" she called, looking for him.

"Call me Fletcher, Lilith," he said, refolding bills to make them lie flat in his pocket.

Lilith hurried up to him. "Daynell is on the phone with your assistant right now. She's so excited she's crying. Oh, I just can't believe it—when I wrote you I never dreamed you'd actually come, much less do anything to help us. I . . . picked out this bracelet. It cost a hundred twenty, with tax. Is that all right?" she asked timidly, presenting her chubby wrist adorned with a gold chain.

"That's fine," Fletcher said, remembering to stop what he was doing to actually look at the jewelry. "Very nice."

"Thank you." Lilith blushed, taking off the stocking cap and shaking out her brown curls. Her cheeks were pink, her eyes glittering—she seemed to be a different woman than the dowdy housewife who had answered the door a few hours ago. After all, an attractive man had just bought her a gold bracelet. Cody looked at her, looked at Fletcher, and then slipped out of the store.

Daniel eschewed a sack for his new toy, ripping open the packaging right away. Jerry grumpily gathered up the trash to dispose of it behind the counter. "I've been working at this store for thirty-five years," he said in a low voice, not speaking particularly to Fletcher. "This store is my world. It's my reason for living. The new owner's got to understand that."

Fletcher regarded him, then turned to Adair. "We're done here. While we go next door to the—what is it?" he interrupted himself to inquire of Lilith.

She was too preoccupied with her bracelet to notice he was talking to her until she glanced up and saw them watching her expectantly. She startled. "Next door? It's the Country Attic Gift Shop."

"Right." Fletcher resumed to Adair, "While we're at the gift shop, would you check back at the jewelry

47

store? Interrupt Daynell long enough to ask Yvonne if she can fish Mulroney's in Beaconville from ol' JB's estate."

"Will do," Adair smiled. "C'mon, Daniel."

He balked when she took his hand, so Fletcher said, "Daniel can come with me." She started out with a nod but he held her back to kiss her lightly on the lips. Noting his wily smile, she assumed things were progressing according to plan.

Adair bundled her coat around her to step out on the icy sidewalk. Two people appeared from nowhere behind her, crossing the street as they talked excitedly about the billionaire in town: "Why d'you think he came here? I bet he's gonna build us a mall!"

"Mall, my foot. If he's from Dallas, he's lookin' for a country getaway. He'll probably put in a ranch and an airstrip."

"Or a casino! They gamble a bunch in Dallas, don't they?"

"I dunno; I think you're thinking of New Jersey."

Uneasy, Adair looked back at them peering in the window of the five-and-dime. Talk about expectations! And for some reason Fletcher seemed to be encouraging them. He was taking a different tack with these people than she'd ever seen, announcing himself and his intentions so publicly. Their sudden enthusiasm for what he could do for them alarmed her a little. They were right to be excited—he was a generous man—but Fletcher's gifts did not come cheaply. He required a cooperation, an alliance, and Adair was not sure they understood that. What might they do when they discovered there were strings attached?

❋ 3 ❋

"**H**i, Yvonne. Adair," she said, after borrowing the receiver from a breathless Daynell.

"Adair, is the weather as bad there as what I've been hearing?" Yvonne asked with her usual businesslike concern.

"Well, it's cold, and icy, but there's nothing coming down right now," Adair said, glancing outside. Daynell, flipping through papers spread out on the counter, suddenly realized something was missing and hurried to the office in the back of the store.

"The forecasts are for more storms in that area. What does Daniel think of all that snow?" Yvonne asked.

"He thinks it's kinda neat. None of it seems to bother him," Adair replied.

"Fletcher isn't spoiling him, is he?" Yvonne asked severely.

Ah yes, Mother Yvonne, Fletcher had been calling her, as she had taken Daniel seriously to heart since the first moment she laid eyes on the scrawny, neglected child. Moreover, she frequently voiced doubts about Fletcher's ability to properly raise children, given his soft heart and widespread interests.

"No more than he's spoiled me," Adair said cheerfully, and Yvonne groaned. "Anyhow, Fletcher wanted me to ask you to buy Mulroney's Five-and-Dime Store from the estate of JB, uh, McConklin of Atlanta. Did you know him?" Adair asked.

"JB? Oh, yes. He and Fletcher crossed swords a number of times. Fletcher made enormous concessions in trying to get him as an ally, but old hardheaded JB just couldn't relinquish control of anything. Then again, he never sold out completely to the Warfield Group, either. I understand they've been looking over his estate, but they haven't been too anxious about it because there were no indications Fletcher had any interest in it," Yvonne said.

"Well, you'd better see if you can buy it quietly then, because this area seems to be shaping up as some kind of battleground. Fletcher said the Warfield Group has practically taken over here already," Adair noted quietly, looking up as Daynell came back from the office with a long form.

"Will do. Where can I get hold of you?" Yvonne asked.

"We're staying at the Best By Far Motel here in Beaconville," Adair replied. "Um, I'm giving you back to Daynell now."

"All right; I'll call you when I've acquired Mulroney's," Yvonne said.

"Thanks. 'Bye." Adair handed the receiver back to Daynell, who immediately began reading some legalese to Yvonne from the long form. *Yvonne's so great. I'd sure hate to be stuck with all that paperwork*, Adair reflected. Thankfully, that is not what Fletcher expected of her. Since he took her and Daniel with him everywhere, she assumed that all he required of her was her presence—for now.

Adair opened the jewelry shop door into the blustery cold outside. Clutching her coat around her, she sighed for some Dallas sunshine. Or better yet, Hawaiian beaches. As she made her way cautiously down the icy sidewalk, she thought back to recent balmy mornings spent watching Daniel scamper along the beach. Suddenly she realized how much he had grown over these past few months.

At that point she looked up to see someone sanding the sidewalk in front of the Country Attic Gift Shop. "It's about time," she fumed to herself. "Somebody's going to fall on this stuff and sue the nearest store's owner for megamillions." And the way things were going, it appeared that owner would be Fletcher—regardless of which shop was sued.

Entering the gift shop, Adair glanced around at cozy afghans folded on chests, baskets of potpourri, and soft sculptures of kittens and geese. Fletcher, holding Daniel, was surrounded by five or six locals intently observing as he closed a verbal deal to buy the store from the elderly owner-manager.

"This is such a load off my heart," the owner, Sophie, was saying, putting a hand to the lace on her high collar. She was slender and delicate, like a dried flower. "I'm just getting too old and tired to put in the hours, but I couldn't simply close it down—this store represents all the retirement I have. Oh, how I've been wanting to be free, to travel, to see something outside of Beaconville! Now that I've found someone willing to buy me out, perhaps I can. . . . But tell me, Mr. Fletcher—"

"Just Fletcher," he interrupted as Daniel shot out his ear—"Pshew! Pshew! Pshew!"—with the toothpick-sized AK-47.

"Fletcher," she amended, continuing, "what is your interest in Beaconville?"

"Lilith wrote me, asking me to come look at your town. I like what I'm seeing. Small-town investments can be profitable, properly managed," he replied. The said Lilith was now beaming like a new Miss America. Cody entered the store with two friends flanking him.

Adair came up, loosening her coat, as this store was kept quite warm. Fletcher paused with a question in his eyes, and she offered, "Yvonne's looking into buying Mulroney's. She'll call us at the motel when she gets it."

Lilith immediately objected, "Mr. Streiker, I won't have you staying at any motel. You come stay with us."

"Fletcher," he reminded her, then accepted with, "Thank you, Lilith," and Adair's heart sank. She was already weary of this cold little town, and lodging in a near stranger's home did not sound all that encouraging.

"Daddy, I'm hungry," whined Daniel on his arm, and Fletcher looked inquiringly at his wife.

"I am, too," she admitted.

"The Little Bangkok Tea Room is just down the street. Cody, have they opened up? Go tell them to open up for Mr. Streiker," Lilith instructed.

"Sure, Mom." Cody and his friends darted out the door and began shoe-skating down the street to Little Bangkok.

Sophie turned her attention to the last few details relating to the sale. "You'll continue to employ Mrs.

Potters, won't you? She's been with me for nearly twenty years," she pressed Fletcher.

"Certainly," he said with a nod to frilly Mrs. Potters, who stood apart respectfully.

"And you won't open for Sunday hours, will you? I find that deplorable," Sophie continued.

"No Sunday hours," Fletcher confirmed.

Sophie turned to her stock then, noting this and that about her merchandise: "The lace must be kept under plastic—I don't allow the packages to be opened until purchased. And the dolls with the sleep eyes mustn't be left on their backs. But Mrs. Potters knows all this." Fletcher nodded with a slight smile as Sophie lovingly smoothed a doll's flaxen curls.

Cody stuck his red face in the door. "Little Bangkok's open."

"Good." Fletcher put Daniel down and Adair took the boy's hand. "C'mon and I'll buy you lunch," Fletcher offered, and everyone standing within earshot took it as a personal invitation.

With a growing entourage, Fletcher and Adair headed down the street to Little Bangkok. The manager opened the door with an apologetic, "I'm sorry; the owner says there's no way he's gonna sell."

"We just want lunch," Fletcher replied mildly, and the manager quickly assured him that lunch was entirely possible. While the buffet was being set up, the guests seated themselves in rings of importance around Fletcher: Lilith and Cody, with his fortunate friends, were closest to the Streikers; next to them were Sophie, Mrs. Potters, and Jerry Hayworth. Jerry was bumped to another table when Daynell arrived and had to be seated close enough to Fletcher to relay her conversation with Yvonne.

"It's all set," Daynell confirmed happily, settling

into the chair on his right. Daniel was on his left, with Adair next to him. "Yvonne faxed me everything I have to sign and notarize, and she'll take care of everything with Delightfully Yours. Mr. Streiker, your terms are just wonderful. This is a dream come true," Daynell gushed.

"Good. I'm glad you're happy," Fletcher said.

Adair listened uneasily. She and he had exchanged identical sentiments their first evening together, and it was all true. But she knew there were speed bumps ahead on this Highway to Happiness that no one here could see yet. Hitting them wrong was liable to be jarring.

By the time the waitresses served their drinks, the buffet was announced ready, which prompted a scramble for the line. The locals were courteous enough to insist that the Streikers help themselves first, so they did.

Adair served Daniel's plate with brown rice, noodles, and carrots, then sat him down so that she could get her own plate. She pretended not to see him dousing his rice with the sugar from several packets.

As Fletcher was looking over the buffet choices behind her, the manager drew him aside. "The owner says he's willing to sell, but only at his price," he whispered, presenting the figure on a slip of paper.

Fletcher glanced at the paper and his brows raised slightly. "He's proud of this place, isn't he? I'll have to try the food before I can tell you whether I'm willing to pay that much." The manager withdrew the paper with an anxious look.

Meanwhile, Adair filled her plate with barbecued pork, rice, and vegetables in a sweet-and-sour sauce. She sat beside Daniel, glancing at the action figure that stood guard over the soy sauce. "Aren't you going to eat? You said you were hungry," she reminded Daniel.

He fidgeted in the vinyl seat, drawing up his legs. "I want some good food. They got no crack seed," he said irritably, referring to a favorite Hawaiian snack.

"They don't have any crack seed," Adair corrected, tugging on his foot to get it off the seat. "You'll just have to wait till we get home for that."

"Then I ain't eatin'," he declared, picking up his toy to exercise it vigorously instead. Adair sighed in mild exasperation, and Fletcher joined them at the table with his plate.

At that time a rather crusty man, forty-five going on sixty, came into the restaurant. He took a plate, letting the manager know he was not with the party already here, and quietly regarded the general hubbub surrounding Fletcher. As the newcomer sat apart from the group to eat, he listened to Daynell and Sophie talk about their new lease on life, and watched as Little Bangkok's manager brought another offer to Fletcher: "He says this is his rock-bottom price."

Fletcher barely glanced at it, saying, "I still haven't tasted everything from the buffet." He hadn't even tasted everything on his plate, as he was being constantly interrupted by someone too excited to notice that he was trying to eat. The manager hurried back to the buffet line to pull some dishes and substitute others.

When the world-weary man had finished his own quick lunch, he came over to Fletcher's table and extended his hand without smiling. "Mr. Streiker, Gus Gramble. I own the hardware store down the street. You'll have to excuse me for asking, but, why are you buying up everything in Beaconville?"

"Because everyone is so anxious to sell to me," Fletcher replied, taking a bite of a cold egg roll.

"Again, you'll have to excuse me; not knowing much

about high finance and such, I tend to ask questions that get people riled. But how do we know your owning everything's going to be good for Beaconville? After all, we have to live here. You don't," Gus observed. Some of those around Fletcher began to look nervous, and Lilith muttered indignantly.

"Look at my track record. Areas where I have a major interest are flourishing," replied Fletcher, unruffled.

"Like where?" Gus pressed.

"It would take me three weeks to run down that list for you. It's all a matter of public record, but you're going to have to do the research yourself, if you're interested," Fletcher said.

Gus appraised him a moment, then said, "I just might do that."

"Good," Fletcher said, meeting his eyes. Gus nodded to himself, turned, and left.

The manager returned to Fletcher's table, plainly nervous. "Mr. Streiker, he says this is his final offer, and my job is on the line if you don't take it," he pleaded with bald honesty.

Surprised, Fletcher asked, "Why is your job on the line?"

"Since I run the place, Mr. Boston says it's my fault if I louse up any opportunities for him," the manager said.

Without even looking at the last figure, Fletcher said, "I suppose I'd better buy it then." The manager smiled sheepishly and a spontaneous murmur of appreciation went around.

"WAH!" Daniel cried suddenly, causing several folks near him to jump. His action figure lay in pieces in his hands—both arms and legs had come apart from the body. "It BROKE! Daddy, it broke!" he wailed. Jerry Hayworth studiously looked away.

"Looks like it," Fletcher agreed mildly.

"Get me another one!" Daniel demanded.

"Why?" Fletcher asked in surprise.

"Because I want another one!" Daniel cried.

"But what if it breaks, too?" Fletcher asked.

"Then get me another one!" Daniel demanded.

They went back and forth like this for a few minutes, Fletcher trying to reason with the stubborn child while Adair silently listened. But all Fletcher's sensible arguments went straight over Daniel's head. He continued to insist on another toy until Fletcher finally said, "No."

"But, Daddy—"

"No."

"Daddy," whined Daniel, heartbroken.

"No." The word was curt and sharp, and to a four-year-old, totally unreasonable. Daniel slumped down in a fit of tears.

Fletcher coolly got up to pay the tab and tip. When he returned to the table, Lilith timidly ventured, "I think there are some other folks who want you to see their shops."

"Sure," he said amiably.

While the group argued about where to take him next, Adair drew Fletcher aside to whisper, "Daniel's tired. Let me take him back to the motel to rest awhile."

"All right," he said, then knelt beside Daniel to help him with his coat. "You go back to the motel with Mommy, okay? I have to do some other stuff, so I need you to take care of Mommy and see that she gets a nap."

Daniel suddenly straightened with responsibility, the toy forgotten. "Okay, Daddy," he said, hugging his neck.

Fletcher stood and ruffled his hair in approval,

then leaned over to kiss her. "I'll come get you when I'm done with *le grand tour*," he murmured. She nodded, glancing at his entourage impatiently standing by. "Jerry, see that Adair and Daniel get back to the motel," Fletcher said before turning out with someone's hand grasping his arm.

"Uh, yeah," Jerry said noncommittally.

When Fletcher had left the restaurant with the others, Jerry turned to Adair and said, "Look, my pickup's parked all the way down behind my store—it'd be just as close for you to walk to the motel. Just cross the street here, cut through the parking lot, go left to the next corner, down three blocks, and you're there."

Adair opened her mouth but Jerry walked on out, leaving her and Daniel standing in the deserted restaurant. For Daniel's sake, Adair swallowed her anger and gripped his hand to start out across the street. Fletcher's entourage had disappeared.

As they walked, Adair noticed that the sky seemed bleaker and heavier than it had been earlier. When they came to the parking lot behind the shops, Adair found that it had not been cleared of snow. Cautiously, she began leading Daniel through it. Daniel, less cautious, slipped on a hidden patch of ice and fell. As she was holding his hand he brought her down, too. Jarred by the sudden contact with rock-hard ice, Adair thoughtlessly uttered an angry exclamation: "Fletcher!"

Daniel scrambled up. "Don't be mad at Daddy, Mommy. I'll help you," he said, earnestly trying to lift her. There certainly wasn't anyone else around to help.

"It's okay, sweetheart," Adair said, getting to her feet. "I wasn't mad at Daddy . . . ," she faltered in trying to reassure him with an untruth. She *was* mad at Fletcher. He knew what people were like, and he knew about people who tried to attach themselves to him for what they could get from him. Why did he allow—encourage—these people to pin all their expectations on him when they were expecting all the wrong things for all the wrong reasons?

At least the anger gave her the energy to hike about six blocks in twenty minutes. Blue and shivering, Adair and Daniel arrived at the motel. She was not happy to discover that they had to stand at the glass doors and ring the bell for entrance; it certainly wasn't like this was the Ritz or anything. The day manager responded with measured speed, and she was finally able to hustle Daniel to their room.

He placidly allowed himself to be relieved of his wet clothes and ushered to the bathroom; but when he realized *she* intended to put *him* to bed, he suddenly came alive and demanded to be taken back out.

"No way. Mr. Fuster says he's cold and needs some cuddling," Adair said, pressing bunny and blankie to his chest as she forcibly tucked them all under the covers.

He grabbed her arm. "Daddy said I had to make you lie down. You have to lie down, too."

"I do, huh?" she sighed, sitting on the edge of the bed to take off her boots.

"Yep," he said solemnly, still holding on to her sleeve.

"For a little while," she murmured, sliding under the covers. Daniel offered her the bunny's backside as he curled up with his knees in her stomach. No doubt about it; he was getting bigger. She gently pushed the knees out of her gut.

"Mommy, I don't like it here. I want to go home," Daniel said softly.

"Me, too. But Daddy's trying to help the people here," she felt obliged to explain, yawning.

59

"But where are the real people? There's nobody real," he complained.

"Nobody real?" Adair quizzed, brows drawn.

"They're not even real," he repeated in scorn, then yawned and burrowed down in the covers.

Adair thought that was a curious comment for a child to make, but as her mind was too foggy to process conversation with a four-year-old, she skipped it and closed her eyes as well.

✳

The warm touch and light breath on her neck were the first wake-up signals she received from the outside world, but they were seamlessly incorporated into her dreams and she did not stir. Then she heard him say softly, "Wake up, Adair. Time to climb out of that coffin."

She tried to roll over, but he pulled the covers off. "Fletcher!" she protested, sitting up. "Where's Daniel?" she asked once she had opened her eyes.

"In the bathroom," Fletcher replied. He leaned down on the bed to whisper, "The first thing we have to do when we get home, definitely, is teach him to sleep in his own bed by himself."

She laughed grumpily, scratching her hair. "*Somebody* tried to tell you that, but you let him make you into a great big Mr. Fuster," she said.

"The Great Fuster," he said, standing as if to present himself.

"MISTER FUSTER!" Daniel exclaimed, running out from the bathroom to leap onto Fletcher. He hugged Daniel, then set him down to zip up his fly for him.

Adair still couldn't motivate herself off the bed, so Fletcher reached down to pull on her hand. "C'mon; you're missing all the fun."

"Yeah, right," she groused, putting her feet to the floor. "What fun?" she asked suspiciously.

"You're looking at the proud owner of approximately eighty percent of Beaconville's downtown businesses," he announced, deadpan.

Adair inhaled, studying him. "Why, Fletcher? These little stores are nothing. I didn't even see you glance at any books. What's so compelling about owning anything in this little town?"

"You said 'little' twice," he observed.

She rolled her eyes. "I didn't mean to be condescending, but—"

"You just meant I shouldn't bother with little stores in a little town," he said.

"I don't see the profit," she said in a hard voice.

Smiling faintly, he drew up the one chair in the room and sat on it backwards to rest his arms on the chair back. "I'm glad you tell me what's on your mind, even when you think it's something I don't want to hear."

"You're good about listening. And then doing something totally unexpected," she admitted.

"Oh, I've looked over some ledgers," he allowed, "though they don't interest me much. I've spent the last three hours looking over other things that have told me a lot more. Books can be cooked, but it's harder to fabricate priorities."

"What in the world do you mean?" she asked.

"Oh, that a windfall like a billionaire blowing into town brings out a person's true agenda. Suddenly you have the opportunity to do whatever you want—are you going to pretend you want one thing when you really want something else?" he asked rhetorically, and Adair shook her head. "Of course not. And that's an important step. The first thing on *our* agenda is to strip away all the pretense. Get down to the truth."

She felt somewhat chastened by the fact that he included her as a partner when she was not much interested in the proceedings. Still, she asked warily, "Then what?"

"Well, let me just skip to the last page here. The fact is, this little trip is going to blow apart the Warfield Group," he said.

Adair startled. "What? How?" Though not understanding the conversation, Daniel was so captivated by this expression that he began acting out explosions across the room.

"All in good time," Fletcher grinned. "Now, if you two can pull yourselves together, we're meeting with all our new employees over at Lilith's house." Fletcher opened his hands to Daniel.

The boy roused from a particularly fierce explosion and raced to his arms, plaintively asking, "Will there be any kids there?"

"I don't know. Maybe," Fletcher replied.

"If there's not, I'm bored," Daniel warned.

"Watch Daddy and you won't be bored," Fletcher promised, winking at Adair as he said it. She pursed her lips skeptically and extracted herself from the bed.

While Adair and Daniel finished dressing, Fletcher paid the room bill. Rather than wait for him in the room, Adair took their bags out to the motel's spartan lobby where Jerry Hayworth sat reading a newspaper.

When he saw her he hastily stood and said, "Uh, sorry about the misunderstanding, Mrs. Streiker. I've got my truck here to take you to Lilith's." He looked so thoroughly chastised that Adair wondered what Fletcher had said to him. Obviously, he found out that Jerry had not driven them to the motel.

"Okay," she said carefully, then looked at the paper in his hands. Just to make conversation, she asked, "Oh, is that the Beaconville paper? May I see it when you're through with it?"

He quickly folded up the slender paper and handed it to her. "Been through with it for a week. It's a weekly, but the edition due out today is late, for the weather."

"Oh. Well, it'll help me get a little history then," Adair feebly laughed. She scanned a front-page column: "Vera Pennington enjoyed her weekend visit to Albright very much. . . . Adele Simms reports that her nephew Jimmy Hollis is coming to see her at the end of January. . . ." Seeing how much the newsprint blackened her hands, she quietly dropped it when Fletcher joined them.

"Sorry it took so long. They were trying to charge me enough to reroof the motel," he said drily, picking up the luggage. He added, "Jerry's got chains on his tires, so he's taking us over to Lilith's." Jerry nodded assent, opening the glass door into the frigid air.

The afternoon had grown progressively bleaker and colder. There was no hint of where the sun might be, nor any indication that there even was a sun in the sky today. After a string of days like this, someone could look up and say, "No light, no warmth— there's no sun. There's never been any sun." If someone else argued that what little light there was had to come from a sun, the skeptic would say, "That's merely a reflection of all our lights bouncing off the clouds." By the springtime, when the sun made its first melting inroads in the snow, such a person would have so firmly established his sunless universe that he would continue to deny the existence of the sun even while soaking up summertime rays on the beach. Adair had known such people.

Fletcher tossed their suitcases into the back of Jerry's pickup on top of numerous bags of sand. With Daniel stubbornly clutching his nylon bag, the Streikers squeezed into the cab and Jerry cranked up the coughing engine to head for Lilith's house. Even with chains on the tires and weight in the back, the pickup fishtailed haphazardly, at one point sliding sideways through a stop sign. Fortunately, no one else was trying to occupy the intersection at the time.

Jerry slid up to Lilith's house and parked generally along the curb, although they could have come to rest twelve inches into the lawn for all they could see. At least he hadn't knocked down the fence—the wooden pickets rose like drowning men above the snowdrifts. Otherwise, the seamless white blanket stretched uninterrupted from the lamppost along the driveway to the barely visible pavement in the center of the street. It had evidently snowed again while Adair and Daniel were resting.

The three of them trudged up to the door and rang the bell (Daniel being carried by Fletcher). Lilith promptly answered: "Hurry on in. Goodness, what a winter! We've got a fire on and hot tea brewing."

"Lilith, that would make my day," Adair admitted, taking off her coat. As long as they were staying here, she was determined to be a gracious guest. And they were welcomed by the hearty blaze in the large, old-fashioned fireplace, and the longhaired cat that watched guardedly from under the coffee table. Daniel barely held still for Adair to unzip his coat before slipping off to woo the beautiful cat once more. Adair followed, stretching out cold hands toward the fire.

"Where are the others?" Fletcher asked Lilith as he took off his hat.

"Oh, you see how bad the streets are. Nobody

thought they could make it over. It's going to take days to get all the paperwork together, anyway. Everybody just agreed that whatever you needed to tell them, you could tell them on the phone. I've got all the numbers here," Lilith chatted, patting a skinny telephone directory on the phone stand. For Fletcher's convenience, she had placed a legal pad and pen next to the telephone and pulled up a chair to the stand.

Fletcher looked at the telephone, shaking his head. "What I've got to tell them has to be in person. You'd better do some calling, Lilith, and let them know that the deal's off for anybody who doesn't make it out here this afternoon. I'll be in front of that fireplace," he said, hanging his coat and hat on a hall rack and exiting to join his family in the next room.

F letcher threw himself down on a big pillow on the floor next to Adair and leaned forward on his elbows. "Let me get you some tea," Adair said, starting to place her cup on the hearth and get up.

He held her arm. "No, thanks, I had about a gallon of it at Little Bangkok."

Adair puckered her lips and nodded. "Then the bathroom's that way."

"I've seen it," he smiled, and they looked over at Daniel on his belly under the coffee table, communicating with the cat. Beyond him, Lilith sat at the phone table earnestly making calls.

Jerry entered the room uncertainly. "Uh, Mr. Streiker, I understand you're wantin' to meet with all the owners, but I don't see exactly how to reach Mr. McConklin." Jerry was from the old school who regarded the wall between employer and employee too formidable to call his new boss by his first name. Either

67

that, or whatever Fletcher had said to him after his failure to transport Adair and Daniel was fresh on his mind.

"No, Jerry; you're the virtual owner of Mulroney's, so you're the one I need to talk to. Sit down," Fletcher said. *Where* was an open question as he himself was stretched out on the floor. After some indecision, Jerry sat on the nubby brown sofa nearby.

Fletcher shifted on his elbow, glancing at Daniel inching closer to the wary cat. "Jerry, you're a good manager. You're reliable, you keep a clean store, and you know your customers," Fletcher began. Jerry nodded in agreement but kept quiet, sensing more to come.

"There's only one change I want you to make. You're to pay up your account with High Five Novelties and not order anything more from them," Fletcher said.

Jerry blinked. "Do you mind telling me why? They're my biggest supplier."

"They exploit child labor overseas who operate dangerous, poorly maintained equipment. They use toxic chemicals in their pigments and smuggle imports to avoid tariffs. Besides all that, they make shoddy toys. Reason enough?" Fletcher asked.

Jerry balked. "All that about kids being maimed by the equipment's just a rumor. Nothing to substantiate it. And I'll give you your money back for the toy your kid broke," he added reluctantly.

"On the contrary, since I'm familiar with several ongoing investigations of this company, I've seen documentation on all of it," Fletcher contradicted him, ignoring the offer of a refund.

"Mind showing me?" Jerry asked.

Fletcher looked up. "Yes, I do. By the time I could collect all the reports and get them to you, they wouldn't be any use to you. You're going to have to decide on the basis of what you already know whether I'm telling the truth."

Jerry sidestepped the issue of what he might already know about High Five's operations. "Even so, any company's gonna have a few production problems," Jerry protested. "If I can't buy from them, who am I supposed to buy from?"

"WonderWorks is a good alternative," Fletcher suggested.

Jerry winced. "Their stuff costs too much."

"I'll accept a smaller profit margin to sell a quality product," Fletcher said.

"That's gonna take," Jerry paused to shake his head in dismay, "that's gonna take some hefty juggling, to replace a major distributor. And six months to sell off the stock I got. None of it's returnable."

"Oh no. You can't sell any more of it at all. Clean it all off your shelves and dispose of it," Fletcher said, shifting back on the pillow.

Now Jerry looked aghast. "Throw it away? That's two-thirds of my store! Do you know what I'll lose on that?"

Fletcher eyed him. "What *you'll* lose? It's my capital, Jerry."

"I. . . ." Jerry looked down in discouragement. "I don't know. . . ."

"The transition might be rough, but you'll be better off in the long run. Trust me on this. Would I be worth what I am if I didn't know something about business?" Fletcher asked, a corner of his mouth curling.

"I don't know," Jerry repeated dully.

"If you don't start on it today, I'll withdraw my offer for Mulroney's," Fletcher warned him.

"I'll have to think it over," Jerry said stiffly, getting

up. With a short nod he walked out.

"He won't do it," Adair predicted, watching over her shoulder as Jerry pulled on his coat and left the house.

"Maybe not," Fletcher said.

"Don't tell me—High Five Novelties is owned by the Warfield Group," she said, turning back to him. The firelight painted his black hair with glints of red.

"Yes, it is, though not even the president of High Five knows it," he responded.

"Fletcher, what will they do when they find out you're here?" she whispered.

"If I'm not mistaken, they already know," he said, looking back to Daniel. The cat was allowing him to lovingly pet her, as long as he kept after her. With each stroke, she would stretch out on the carpet, drawing away by inches until she was just out of reach. Then she would gaze back at him until he scooted forward on his knees to pet her again. "Just like a woman," Fletcher muttered.

"Pardon?" Adair said.

The doorbell rang; Fletcher looked over as Lilith put down the phone and went to answer it. Wrapped in fur, Daynell entered. She barely greeted Lilith before catching sight of Fletcher in front of the fireplace. "Mr. Streiker, when Lilith called I just put on my treads and came right over," she declared, panting. Smiling, Adair looked down at the bulky boots beneath the elegant fur. And for the second time she noted the reluctance to accept a new boss on a first-name basis, even at his invitation.

"Good, Daynell. Sit down," Fletcher said.

She too hesitated before sitting on the nubby sofa, then asked timidly, "So what did you think of my little store?"

Still spread full-length on the floor, Fletcher leaned back on his elbow with his back to the fire. "Daynell," he said, "you're selling good merchandise at a fair price. Your store is very nicely laid out and you treat your customers well. All that is remarkable, considering the problems you've been having with Delightfully Yours."

"True," Daynell laughed nervously.

"I only have one requirement of you before we close the deal," he said, and paused.

"Yes?" Daynell asked with worried brow.

"You have to fire your husband. He's tapping the till," Fletcher said.

"Ohh." Daynell closed her eyes and leaned forward in despair, murmuring, "I was afraid of that. Well . . . as soon as I get through this inventory—"

Fletcher was shaking his head. "It has to be done today, or all bets are off."

"Today?" Daynell gasped. "But—oh, Mr. Streiker— we've been married twenty years!"

"I didn't say you had to divorce him. Just fire him," Fletcher said. She opened her mouth with a helpless stare and he reiterated, "If you don't let me know that it's done today, I'll have Yvonne drop you back in the lap of Delightfully Yours." Daynell looked off in bewilderment at her dilemma, then absently gathered her fur coat about her and left the house without another word.

Adair checked on Daniel under the table, who had persuaded the cat into his arms. Fletcher shifted to reach the poker and shove embers back under the logs. "How familiar this all sounds," she observed, and he looked at her. "How I struggled with having to choose you over ballet. Isn't there some way you can tell them that the choice is just an—an illusion? That if they do what you ask, they'll have everything, and more?"

His smile was subdued as he replaced the poker and leaned closer to her. "At the point of making a choice, would you have believed that? Would you have been able to make the choice without being willing to give up ballet forever?" he asked in a murmur.

She glanced away in some confusion. "I guess not."

"It's not so much an illusion as a—well, a change in focus. A realignment of vision. Then you can see that you've lost nothing at all." His voice dropped to a low growl, and Adair impulsively kissed his beautiful lips.

Someone cleared a throat, and they looked up at Lilith standing in the doorway. "I called everybody. Jerry was already here and Daynell came, you know. Um, Tige Boston—the owner of Little Bangkok—said there's no way he's coming over here this afternoon."

"I'll give him until tomorrow morning to change his mind," Fletcher said, nodding.

"And poor Sophie just burst into tears. She lives over her shop, you know, and doesn't have a car, and just didn't know how in the world she was going to make it over here," Lilith continued anxiously.

"That's too bad," Fletcher said in unconcern, stretching before the fire. Lilith shifted in the doorway and the Persian wriggled free of Daniel's grasp to come rub against her leg. Daniel followed on all fours.

Lilith looked down at him and smiled. "Do you like my kitty cat?"

"Uh-huh," Daniel admitted, petting her against Lilith's leg.

"I think she likes you, too. Do you know what her name is? We call her Sphinx, because she looks just like a sphinx when she sits on the mantel surveying her domain," Lilith said.

"What's a mantel?" Daniel said dubiously.

"Here. Right here." Lilith walked over and patted

the roughhewn mantel cluttered with knickknacks. "It's the funniest thing you ever saw, to see her perch up here like she's queen and watch everybody." Sphinx, taking offense, sauntered with dignity out of the room, tail held high. Daniel continued to sit on the floor, looking forlorn.

"I just made some cheese popcorn last night. Would you like some?" Lilith asked.

"If it's good," Daniel said with cautious optimism, getting up to follow her into the kitchen.

Adair smiled, then turned to Fletcher to ask, "What if Sophie can't get here?"

"Oh, she can if she wants to. If she won't make the effort to come to me, she won't be motivated to do what I ask," he said lazily. Speaking of effort, he expended a little himself to get up and put another log on the fire.

The doorbell rang again, and Lilith left Daniel in the kitchen with a huge bowl of popcorn to answer it. Adair and Fletcher waited expectantly, and a moment later Gus Gramble appeared in the den doorway. Adair was surprised at first—he was the owner of the hardware store who had confronted Fletcher in the restaurant.

Fletcher waited without speaking as Gus took off his lumberjack hat and smoothed back his thin gray hair. "Mr Streiker," he began in a tone of adversarial respect, "Jerry just told me about the demands you made on him to buy the place, and I suspect you've got a list for the others, too. I knew that was gonna happen, and I tried to tell them that they didn't know what they were getting into. They wouldn't listen then, but they're liable to listen now. So I'm here to tell you to your face that if you keep meddling with our businesses and our livelihoods, it's gonna get nasty. I suggest you just take your money and your family back to the big city and forget about Beaconville."

Her hackles rising, Adair felt strongly inclined to take his suggestion. But Fletcher demanded, "Did you do what you said you were going to do?"

Gramble looked caught off guard. "Do what?" he asked.

"Did you research me? Did you look up my corporation and find out what I've done?" Fletcher persisted.

"Ah . . . with the roads as bad as they are—" Gus began making excuses for not having done the research.

"You don't have to go any farther than the library. But if you want to threaten me properly, you'd better find out all you can about me, don't you think?" Fletcher asked. He allowed a measured pause for Gus's stare, then predicted, "Before I leave, you'll jump to get on board with me."

Straightening, Gus responded, "That'll be a cold day in hell, Mr. Streiker." He turned on his heel and left with a bang of the front screen door.

"That's exactly what it is," muttered Fletcher, turning back to the fire, and Adair studied him in slight apprehension.

After a few seconds of thought, he got up and went to the telephone stand. Picking up the receiver, he placed a collect call to a Dallas number. A moment later he said, "Hi, Yvonne. How's it going with Mulroney's? Uh-huh. Okay, put a hold on that until you hear from me. I want you to do something else— I want to know everything there is to know about Gus Gramble, Tige Boston, and Max Beene—all Beaconville people. I especially want to know if they have any significant others who live outside Beaconville. Got that? What? No, what about Sugar?" He listened a moment, then said, "Okay. We're staying at Lilith's house now, so I'll call you."

When he had come back to the den and dropped down on the floor beside her, Adair asked, "What's that about Sugar?" Fletcher's former housekeeper was a special friend to both of them.

Fletcher rubbed his face in agitation. "Her arthritis is acting up again and she's trying to keep it a secret—she doesn't want to 'bother' me about it. If she won't break down and admit she's in pain, I'm just going to have to knock her out, put her in the hospital, and have them do the reconstructive surgery without her consent."

Adair winced. "Poor Sugar."

"Either way it's gonna hurt, but I'm not going to let her suffer forever like that," he said testily. He himself sounded hurt at Sugar's attempt to carry this burden on her own.

Mindful of this, Adair turned to the subject of Gus's threats: "You don't have to convince me that you know what you're doing, but . . . do you really want Daniel here while you incite a mob?"

He smiled slightly. "Daniel's not in any danger. Neither are you. But I want you to take notes here, and Daniel goes with his parents. That's all."

She understood him. It seemed like every experience he had led her through since last October was designed to reinforce her trust of him, usually by requiring what at first seemed incomprehensible. Now he was initiating the same kind of relationship with these people. Viewed objectively, of course it made sense to require that Daynell fire her dishonest husband or Jerry stop patronizing an unscrupulous supplier. But to them, it was tantamount to asking them to fly.

The only possible drawback in his plan was that Adair simply didn't care that much. Nothing about these people excited an immediate desire to inconvenience herself too much for them. She felt rather detached from their decisions—it certainly wasn't a matter of life and death to *her*. Although she was honest enough to admit this to herself, she didn't try to explain it to Fletcher.

The telephone rang and Lilith answered it. "Good, I'm so glad," she expressed in relief to the calling party, then hung up and came to tell Fletcher, "That was Sophie. She found someone to drive her over."

"Good," he replied vaguely, staring into the fire, and Lilith quietly withdrew to the television room.

"Hey, how do you know Gus Gramble will 'hop on board' with you? Or did you say that just to make him mad?" Adair asked, nudging his shoulder with hers.

He dropped his head in light laughter, shielding his face from the heat of the flames. But before he answered, the doorbell rang and Lilith admitted another man whom Adair did not know. This guy stalked straight into the room with an Attitude. He did not sit. "Okay, Mr. Streiker, just out of curiosity, what do you expect me to do with my shop?" he demanded.

"Nothing, Max," Fletcher replied, barely glancing over his shoulder.

This was definitely not what Max had expected to hear. "Nothing?" he asked suspiciously.

"Not a thing," Fletcher said.

"You mean, you'd let me run it as is?" Max asked in wary hope.

"Not hardly," Fletcher said drily, turning toward him. The fire danced behind his head, providing a disconcerting aura. "I'd raze it and set you up in an entirely different business."

Max was too appalled to reply at first, then his eyebrows drew down and he spat, "Over my dead body.

You keep your offers, Mr. Big Shot. I'm with Gus and Jerry—ain't no way you're gonna waltz in and take over our town without a heck of a fight on your hands!" With that promise, he stalked out.

Alarmed, Adair asked Fletcher, "What business does he own?"

"The bookstore," Fletcher answered.

"What is he doing wrong?" she wondered.

"He isn't doing anything wrong; he's making a nice profit. But the stuff he's selling eats up souls like acid," Fletcher said calmly, and she stared at him. He looked around. "Do we know where Daniel is?"

Adair's gaze snapped and she got up. "I'll find him," she said.

She looked in the kitchen, but he wasn't there. Then she looked into the small television room and saw him lounging in a recliner with a huge bowl of cheese popcorn in his lap. The television was turned on to a steamy soap opera in which the female lead was disrobing seductively. Lilith sat on a nearby couch, watching intently while occasionally helping herself to the popcorn.

"Uhhh," Adair stammered, checking her impulse to turn off the television. "Enough popcorn, Daniel. You need to come in here with Daddy and me." She handed the bowl to Lilith and pulled him out of the chair.

"Wait a second," he balked, eyes on the screen.

"No. Come now," Adair insisted, dislodging him from the chair.

"I don't want to!" Daniel shouted, yanking back against her grip.

"Shh," Lilith admonished from the couch.

"Excuse us," Adair said with gritted teeth. Daniel wailed in protest as she lifted him bodily from the recliner and started carrying him from the room.

Suddenly she stopped, staring at something on the floor. It was a white stuffed dog with a red bow. What startled Adair was that it looked exactly like one she had been given when she was six, right down to the purposefully frayed ends of the bow.

She let Daniel down, and he turned back to the show. Hesitantly, Adair picked up the dog to check its fur. A large chunk of it was missing from the dog's side, right where she had spitefully cut it.

"Lilith, where did you get this?" Adair asked, showing her the small toy animal.

Lilith glanced back. "At a garage sale."

"How"—Adair gulped—"how did the fur get cut on it?"

"Some child playing with scissors, I suppose. It was only fifty cents. Please be quiet—this is my favorite show." Lilith settled in the recliner to watch her show, and Adair dropped the dog to drag Daniel out.

"I want Mr. Fuster," Daniel whined, so she took him to the bottom of the stairs where their luggage sat. Daniel studiously dug through his bag for friend Fuster while Adair watched with pounding heart.

That dog—it couldn't be the same one. That was impossible. But seeing one so like it inflamed the feelings of anger and shame associated with the original. It had been given to her by a friend of her father's who had tried to molest her. Recalling the disturbing ideas he had introduced to her, his lustful smile, and his unwelcome hands—Adair had taken the scissors to bed with her one night as protection and used them on the dog instead. When her mother had come in and caught her destroying the toy, she had scolded, "You ungrateful, destructive girl! You go apologize to Mr. Howell right now!" Adair would never forget his indulgent smile at her defiant apology.

And what had become of the dog? Adair could not remember. Even if it had found its way to this house, it wouldn't look so new after eighteen years. Just a coincidence—some other child had taken her anger out on a stuffed animal. Adair blocked out the mystery to herd Daniel and Mr. Fuster back to the den where Fletcher was.

Sophie had just now arrived, bundled up in a black wool coat and muffler. After answering the door again, Lilith had returned to the television room and emphatically closed it off. Sophie was accompanied by a rather blank-faced young man with long hair and a beard, whom she introduced as Mrs. Potters's son Joshua. "He brought me on his snowmobile—a terrifying ride," she added with an apprehensive glance at Fletcher.

"Glad you could make it, Sophie," Fletcher said with perhaps not enough gravity at her ordeal. "Sit down."

Like everyone else who had accepted the invitation, she sat on the sofa. Joshua lolled by the door. "I understand you've certain requirements of those you do business with," she opened stiffly, removing her gloves.

"Yes," he confirmed.

"So what is it you require of me?" she asked. She folded her gloves in her lap and lifted her chin to await the answer.

Fletcher shifted. His eyes were somewhat bloodshot from the smoke of the fire, and he rubbed them almost as if he was stalling. Sophie waited, her chin elevated. "For now," he finally said, "I ask only that you continue to run the Country Attic as you have in the past."

She blinked several times. "You want me to stay on at the store and run it?"

"Yes," he said.

"That's all?" she asked.

"For now," he repeated.

"And what later, Fletcher?" she asked, the first one to call him by his first name.

"Eventually, Sophie, I'll want you to leave Beaconville and come work for me elsewhere, probably in Dallas," he said.

She looked surprised, flattered, and reluctant. "Why, I did want to travel some—I've been feeling restless and I don't know why—but I don't know . . . I'm not very strong. I might not be able to do the work you require."

"Yes, you can," Fletcher assured her.

"And if I don't wish to come?" she asked.

"I'm certainly not going to make you. But it would be worth your while," he said in his classic manner of understatement.

"Well, I. . . ." She hesitated, and Adair found herself holding her breath. Was there any way to tell this sweet old lady that the opportunity of a lifetime lay at her feet? "May I continue to employ Mrs. Potters?" she asked.

"I already told you that you could," he reminded her.

"Well . . . as hard as I'm trying, I can't find anything unreasonable in what you ask. I will continue to work at the store," she agreed, standing to offer her hand.

Fletcher stood up to take it. "Thank you, Sophie."

"I should be thanking you, Fletcher," she observed, and he smiled back in a way that said, *That's true*. "Joshua," she nodded to her companion, who detached himself from the doorway and shuffled over to open the front door for her.

On their way out, Adair heard Sophie say, "And *please* slow down around the corners, Joshua!"

Adair turned excitedly to Fletcher. "Somebody's actually cooperating with you! I don't believe it!"

"Yeah," he laughed lightly, running a hand over his brow.

"Are you all right?" she asked. He looked drained.

"Yeah, sure," he said, glancing toward the television room where Lilith sat engrossed in a late-afternoon talk show.

Daniel came wandering back from looking for the cat. "Daddy, this place is dead," he complained, adding, "I'm hungry."

"Okay. There's a—we passed a fast-food restaurant not far from here," Fletcher answered somewhat distractedly. "Let's go see what they've got." He cracked the door and leaned into the television room. "Lilith—?"

"Shh!" she replied without looking up.

"I guess Lilith doesn't want anything to eat right now," Fletcher said, and Adair inwardly observed, *She's sure not putting herself out to make sure her guests get anything, either.*

"Let's go," Fletcher said, going to the hall rack for their coats.

They got bundled up for the short walk and let themselves out the front door. The sun, having abandoned any attempt to break through the barrier of clouds, was now in full retreat before the gloom. After taking three steps down the slippery, snowy sidewalk, Daniel raised his arms to his father, who picked him up. They trudged down the street toward the faint lights of the corner hamburger joint. It was only two blocks down, but those two blocks seemed like mile-long stretches.

Shivering, Adair peeked out from her upturned coat collar and stopped dead. The house in front of her, with its lopsided shutters and rigid row of junipers— "Fletcher!" she gasped, flailing for him. "That house! I know that house! That's Old Man Brunley's house!"

5

Fletcher glanced back at Adair as she stood staring at the malevolent house. Old Man Brunley had lived a few blocks over from her when she was about eight—in Euless, hundreds of miles from here. He was a nice, quiet old man who lived by himself and never bothered anybody. Being somewhat infirm, he couldn't keep up the maintenance on his house very well, so occasionally the neighbors would pitch in to help him paint the woodwork or clean the gutters. The adults liked him because he always smiled and said hello, but the children all agreed he was creepy and stayed away from him.

Adair had been in his house only once, when her mother took a casserole to him after he'd suffered a bad fall. Staring at this house now, Adair vividly recalled the terror she had felt when her mother left her alone in the front room while she took the casserole to the kitchen. It was just a room, with walls and furniture, but to the eight-year-old it was full of death. That's what she remembered thinking: the house was full of death.

Some time after that, police from across the country came and knocked on his door, and they took Old Man Brunley away. He went up on charges of murdering his wife and her parents twenty-five years before, and was convicted. For twenty-five years he had been hiding those murders under a facade of meekness, growing old with the guilt still hanging over him. Shortly afterwards, Adair's family had moved out of that neighborhood.

"Mommy!" Daniel called urgently from Fletcher's shoulder halfway up the block. "Mommy, come on!"

Shivering fiercely, Adair hurried to catch up with them. "That house—," she stammered, grasping Fletcher's elbow to pull herself close to him, "that house looks just like one that a murderer lived in. He lived down the street from us," she said through chattering teeth.

Fletcher didn't reply to her ravings, merely raising his face as they neared the hamburger joint. He reached out and yanked on the door to let themselves in.

Though warm, the restaurant was empty of customers, and for a while it looked empty of employees as well. The Streikers went up to the counter to study the menu hanging above the cash register. Distracted, Adair only glanced at the choices of deluxe burger, giant burger, hungry man doubleburger, and so on. "I'll just have a burger," she mumbled.

"That looks like what we'll all have," Fletcher replied. "Hello?" he called.

They heard a rustle as a sullen counter attendant shuffled up and picked up a pen, wordlessly waiting for their order. "Three hamburgers," Fletcher said.

The attendant looked up with languid scorn. "*Which* burgers?" he queried, pointing up to the choices with his pen.

Fletcher glanced at the menu. "Three deluxe burgers."

"You coulda said that the first time," the attendant grumbled. "What all you want on those?"

Fletcher glanced up again, where the menu advised that the deluxe burger came loaded with lettuce, tomatoes, and pickles. "Everything that's supposed to be on them," he said. Adair, feeling slightly faint in the warmth of the restaurant, sat down at a table.

"You want lettuce, tomatoes, and pickles on all three?" the attendant asked dubiously.

"If it's convenient," Fletcher said with a sober face.

The order-taker returned to his pad. "You want super sauce on those?"

"No," Fletcher said.

"The super sauce is our specialty," the attendant argued.

"If it's that important to you, then put it on," Fletcher said.

"You want fries?" the attendant continued down his checklist.

"No," said Fletcher, reaching into his pocket for some cash. Daniel put his head down on Fletcher's shoulder.

"Drinks?" the attendant droned on.

"Two mediums and one small cola," Fletcher said, searching for something less than a hundred-dollar bill. Clued by the attendant's disgusted sigh, he quickly scanned the list of choices on the soda fountain. "Two medium Dr. Fizz and one small orange."

The attendant rang up the order. "That'll be eight ninety-five," he said, and Fletcher gave him a twenty.

After making change, he drew the drinks and shuffled back to the grill to start on the burgers.

Adair watched him from her table, still trying to recover from the shock of seeing Old Man Brunley's house. This attendant's attitude was all too familiar from her few years working at the bank. That is, he hated his job. He hated taking orders, cooking patties, making change, and mopping floors. He hated the stupid uniforms and the stupid customers. He hated everything about it, but he was stuck here because he needed a job.

Fletcher paused at the counter with the drinks on a tray and Daniel hanging limply on his shoulder. Then he startled Adair by inviting the attendant, "If you want to do something different for a living, come work for me."

The burger-flipper glanced up from the grill with a sarcastic, "Right."

Fletcher said no more, picking up the tray with his free hand and turning to the table where Adair waited. She sat holding her head in dismay, feeling a vague urge to leap over the counter and shake the attendant by his limp shoulders. *Are you crazy? Why won't you listen to him? Wake up!*

Fletcher sat across the table from her, gently relocating Daniel to the plastic seat beside him. Adair took the drinks from the tray and Fletcher placed it on a nearby table. He took off his beautiful hat to place it upside down on the table behind them. Adair, her head pounding and her hands cold, watched Daniel leaning on his daddy to sip his orange drink through the straw.

She began to relax a little, regarding him. He hardly looked like the same child who had recoiled in terror at the mere mention of Fletcher's name. Now Daniel could travel anywhere in perfect confidence, even to a cold, strange town, as long as he was with his daddy.

Adair knew she needed to take a lesson from Daniel's book. Although she didn't particularly want to come and liked it less the longer they were here, she realized that Fletcher had good reasons for coming. Arguing with him about it was not productive. Still, she felt she should tell him her misgivings.

So haltingly, she began, "I know I must not be making any sense—it just startled me to see that house. Of course it's not his house—there must be hundreds built about the same time that all look like that. And then, before that, I saw this toy dog that Lilith has—it looks just like one I had when I was little, and it did not bring back happy memories to see it."

He glanced at her without replying. Adair wasn't sure what she wanted him to say—maybe just a reassurance that she wasn't imagining things.

The door opened with a blast of cold air, and they looked over to see Cody and his two friends come in. "Hey, Fletch," Cody greeted him casually, as if they were old pals. "You wanna buy us some burgers, doncha?" He was sorely afflicted with the common teenage curse of needing to impress his friends.

"Sure, Cody. I'll buy your dinner," Fletcher said.

"Cool." Cody swaggered to the counter where the attendant waited listlessly with his pen. "Okay, give me a hungry man, double fries, a large Dr. Fizz, and a popover," Cody ordered.

The second boy chided him, "That all you eating? Hey, I need two hungry mans and a deluxe, three fries, and four popovers."

The third boy, a head taller than Cody and twice as thick, caught on to a great game. "You're both Herbs. I need *five* giants, *ten* fries, a gallon of Dr. Fizz, and your girlfriend!" They broke into hoots of laughter as the counter attendant took it all down with a straight face. Then the second boy decided he was hungrier than he thought, and upped his order. So did Cody.

By the time they had finished reordering several times to top each other, Cody brought a ticket for $73.81 to Fletcher. The other two boys, not to mention Adair, watched to see what he would do while Cody waited with a smirk.

Fletcher reached into his pocket, remarking, "You guys seem to be really hungry tonight."

"Haven't eaten in weeks," Cody cracked with a wink at his buddies.

"Even if you managed to eat all that," Fletcher went on, pulling out a hundred-dollar bill, "you'd still be hungry again by tomorrow, wouldn't you?"

He held the bill out to Cody, who took it with an expression of hilarity: "Yeah, so we'll just meet you here, same time tomorrow!"

His friends cracked up. Fletcher waited for them to quiet down as Cody took the bill to the counter. The attendant made change, then placed the Streiker's food order on the counter. "Number twenty-three," he called in perfect seriousness.

"That must be you." Cody looked back over his shoulder at Fletcher and his family.

"Will you bring that to me?" Fletcher asked casually. Cody paused. The really cool response would have been to sneer, *What, do I look like I work here?* and his pals were waiting to guffaw over such a line.

With the words on his lips, Cody suddenly thought about talking with his father today for the first time in ten years, and thought about who had made that possible. The sarcastic question died unspoken. With an aloof jerk of his head, Cody took the tray of burgers with one hand and brought it to Fletcher's table. His two buddies looked crestfallen. "Thanks," Fletcher said, taking burgers from the tray.

Cody then looked down at the cash wadded up in his hand, but Fletcher did not. Obviously he didn't care about it—the man's a billionaire, right? What did he want with a few bucks? So why shouldn't Cody keep it? Heaven knows he needed it a lot more than a billionaire did.

Adair watched from the corner of her eye to see what Cody would do with the cash. He stared down at it, then drew up as though inspired by a new thought. Deliberately laying the cash on the table next to Fletcher, he asked quietly, "Can you get my dad to come here?"

Fletcher eyed him as he repocketed the cash. "I won't be here for long," he said in almost a whisper. "When I leave, I want you to come with me."

Cody gazed at him, then blinked. "What about my dad? I told him to come here."

"Your dad will never come here. You'll have to leave to see him," Fletcher said.

Cody's breathing quickened and his friends looked over curiously. "What's going on, jag?" asked the bigger, more aggressive one.

Buckling under the disapproval of his friends, Cody shrugged carelessly and went over to sit with them at a table across the room. The Streikers unwrapped their burgers and began eating. Daniel took two bites of burger and then dismantled it to remove the pickles. Fletcher then had to help him put it back together. Fidgeting, Daniel took one more bite before lying across the seat with his feet in Fletcher's lap. Adair could hardly eat half her burger, as her stomach was already knotted with restlessness and apprehensions. After finishing his burger, Fletcher sat crumpling and smoothing out the wrapper—waiting to talk further with Cody, Adair guessed.

In a few minutes the restaurant worker began bringing out the boys' order. They wolfed down the first several burgers, being genuinely hungry, but when they were stuffed to the gills and the burgers kept coming, they started grinding them in each other's faces, stomping on them, and tossing them at targets across the dining room. Noting this, Daniel picked up his unfinished burger as if to throw it. Adair grabbed the little fist and uttered, "Don't you dare, mister." Meanwhile, Fletcher said not a word and Adair began seething.

When several burgers began sailing their way and one knocked Fletcher's new hat to the floor, Adair eyed him and quietly begged, "Will you please say something to them?"

Only then did he lean back in his seat and look over at the boys. They looked back, snickering. "I guess I made a mistake, buying your dinner," he observed drily. They looked at each other to see who could think of a good comeback. The attendant was still bringing out food. "I'm not usually wrong," Fletcher said, eyes locked on Cody. The message was clearly: *I know you're not who you're pretending to be*.

Cody's friends were still trying to think of a clever response. "You must be reality impaired, pop," was the best the bigger guy could articulate. But Cody wasn't looking at his friends anymore, as the pull from Fletcher's direction was almost magnetic.

The attendant finished bringing out the food, which filled up a second table. Then he mechanically began cleaning up greasy messes from the floor, as if customers always ordered a bunch of food to splatter it around the restaurant. Looking around at the ridiculous waste, Cody suddenly flushed in shame.

The big guy had begun to toss a burger up to the slowly rotating ceiling fan, trying to hit the blades, when Cody snatched it from his hands. "Cut it out," Cody demanded.

"You don't dis me, Herb," the boy growled, but Fletcher's level stare from across the room unnerved him somewhat. "This is cheesy. Let's jet." He jerked his head toward the other kid, who looked suddenly ready to leave.

Those two banged out of the doors into the frosty twilight, leaving Cody sitting awkwardly in the midst of food variously spoiled and still edible. After a moment, Cody turned self-consciously toward Fletcher and muttered, "I'm sorry." Fletcher nodded slightly in acknowledgment of his apology without offering any assuagement.

"I guess . . . ," Cody began in chagrin, eyeing the restaurant worker sweeping up smashed burgers into a dustbin. Then he dropped to all fours to help clean them up. Although Fletcher appeared not to be watching, Adair knew he was aware of Cody's every move.

When the ruined food was disposed of, there were still piles of it overflowing two tables. Cody approached Fletcher's table and said, "I don't know what to do about all that. I can't give it back."

Fletcher looked up. "Do you know of anyone who'd want it?"

Cody shifted his eyes, thinking, then a light came on. "Yeah, sure! The Twilight Trails Community Center is just a few blocks down—those old geezers would go bonkers over some burgers and fries." Inspired by this idea, he ordered several large bags from the attendant and packed up the rest of the food.

Hoisting his sweatshirt hood, Cody gathered up the bags and headed out the door. He paused to tell Fletcher,

"I'll tell 'em they're from you." Fletcher nodded.

After Cody had left, Fletcher leaned back in his seat and breathed with relish, "Got him. He's going with us."

Adair shifted uneasily. "Fletcher, is that a good idea? What about his school and his home? What will Lilith say?"

"I'm going to get Lilith to come, too. Um, I'd better tell you that anybody who wants a future has got to leave this place. That's really why I've come, Adair—to get anybody we can to leave," Fletcher said.

Adair blinked. "Then why are you buying their businesses?"

"Eventually, to persuade them to leave. In that respect, Gus Gramble is absolutely right," Fletcher said, draining the last of his cola. "I'd shut down the whole town if they'd let me."

Adair's jaw dropped. "Shut down the whole town—! I don't understand. Why don't you just help them improve the quality of life here?"

"It will never be better here, Adair—the Warfield Group is too entrenched. The only hope for these people is to leave. The problem is, they can't get out on their own. They don't even know it's possible to leave, and wouldn't consider it if I didn't come pry them out," Fletcher said.

Adair felt dizzy again. "You're not making any sense at all. This is beginning to scare me."

Fletcher looked outside. "It's snowing again. We'd better get back to Lilith's."

They bundled up again and Daniel climbed back into Fletcher's arms. Fastening every button on her coat, Adair braced for the icy blast as Fletcher shoved open the door.

They hustled down the sidewalk in the early-evening

snowfall. The monotony of the grayness and bone-chilling cold lodged in Adair's gut. Fletcher walked so quickly carrying Daniel that she had to trot to keep abreast of him. "Then you're just giving up this town to the Warfield Group? I thought you said you were going to blow them apart," she said at his side.

"That's right, and anybody still here when that happens is going to get burned," Fletcher said grimly. Adair sighed at his riddles. But she kept her head down to avoid looking at Old Man Brunley's house as they passed it.

The snow began coming down harder, so that every time she looked up she caught a face full of little cold darts. She could not even see across the street to ascertain which two-story house was Lilith's. But Fletcher's stride was confident, so she held his arm and let him lead her.

Fletcher turned up an invisible walk and they went through the front gate, still frozen half-open. He led up to the door and rang the bell, but did not wait for Lilith before opening the door himself.

They stood in the foyer, shaking off snow and stamping their feet. "Lilith?" Fletcher called.

Some moments later she came out from the den, a tentative expression on her face. "We went out for a burger. Anyone come by while we were gone?" Fletcher asked cordially.

"No, no one came," Lilith answered vaguely.

"Then who called?" Fletcher asked.

"Well . . . ," Lilith hedged, "several. Daynell, for one. She's just so upset. She doesn't see how in the world she can fire her husband. She's pleading for you to reconsider."

"I'm afraid there's no room for negotiation on that point," Fletcher said, pitiless.

"But what's Powell supposed to do for a living? What if he gets desperate?" Lilith asked fearfully.

"I sure hope he gets desperate enough to come talk to me about it," Fletcher replied.

"Oh my," Lilith breathed, regarding him uncertainly. Her second thoughts about him were broadcast all over her face. Suddenly realizing that, Lilith smoothed her face and laughed nervously. "Well, you've certainly stirred up our little town. Come on upstairs and let me show you your room."

"Thank you, Lilith," Fletcher replied. Daniel was throwing himself around in tiredness.

Lilith led the way upstairs to a guest bedroom furnished with an old four-poster bed and dresser. She was pointing out the bathroom across the hall when they heard the front door open and Cody's voice call, "Mom!"

"Be right down!" she called down the stairs, then turned to say, "You make yourselves right at home now."

"Thank you, Lilith." Adair tried to smile. Nodding distractedly, Lilith went on down the stairs.

Fletcher ran a hand down Adair's back and murmured, "I'm going downstairs to talk to them. Be back up in a while." She nodded, almost curious enough to drag Daniel back down so she could listen in.

But, bowing to duty, she took Daniel to the bathroom and began running water in the large old tub. The wooden baseboards around the tub were rotted through, as was the framing around the small frosted window at eye level. Adair hoped the wood underneath the tub was in better shape.

Clumsy with weariness, Daniel began undressing himself. "I can do it by myself, Mommy," he said irritably when her hands itched to hurry him along.

"All right," she said, forcing patience. When he was

done, she lifted him over the high edge of the tub into the warm water. Then she realized she had left his nightclothes in the other room. "Be right back, Daniel," she said, standing.

But he leaped up from the tub, screaming, "Don't leave me!"

"Daniel!" Adair caught him as he slipped on the smooth porcelain, before he could bang his face on the edge of the tub.

"Don't leave me!" he cried, grasping her arms with stubby fingers.

"Daniel, I—I was just going to get your jammies. It's okay; we'll get them after you're done. It's all right. I'll stay here with you," she reassured him, lowering him back to the warm water. The wild expression in his eyes subsided, but he watched her every move while she bathed him, then demanded to get out the instant she was done.

Adair wrapped him in the old, faded bath-towel hanging on the wooden dowel nearby and carried him to the guest room. "My goodness," she murmured, rubbing him down, "what was that all about? You acted as though I was going to let you drown or something."

"You don't leave me alone," he scolded, bending for bunny and blankie in his nylon bag in spite of her efforts to get his nightshirt on. He gathered his friends close to his face and eyed her reproachfully. "My other mommy might snatch me away," he said.

Adair's hands faltered holding up his pajama bottoms. This was the first time he had ever spoken of Sandra to her, and it was disconcerting that it should come while they were so deep in enemy territory. "Here, Daniel? While you're with us? Why do you say that?" she asked.

Climbing into her lap, he said, "'Cause I saw her."

·6·

A dair's mouth instantly dried to dust. "Daniel . . . are you sure? Are you sure you saw your first mommy, Sandra?"

"Uh-huh." He nodded from her arms.

"When, Daniel?" Adair asked.

"When you and me went walking to the room and you fell down," Daniel said.

"I didn't see anyone! Where was she?" Adair asked.

"In a window. Watchin' from a window," Daniel said.

A hint of skepticism surfaced as she observed, "But . . . you didn't say anything. You didn't seem scared."

"I had to take care of you," he said, looking up at her, and Adair closed her eyes to squeeze the little man.

"It's all right, Daniel. We won't let anyone snatch you. We'll tell Daddy about it as soon as he comes back upstairs," Adair said. By now she was convinced that he had merely seen someone who looked like Sandra.

This claustrophobic little town was a natural breeding ground for one's worst nightmares.

Placated, Daniel spread his blankie to find a suitable corner already twisted and stiffened into the proper shape. Adair grimaced as he contentedly stuffed the blankie corner into his mouth. It was enough of a battle to get the blankie away just for washings; Adair didn't feel up to waging the war necessary to wean him from it entirely.

She turned out the room light (but left on the hall light) before coming back to rock him and sing "Jesus Loves Me," his favorite bedtime song. Then she tucked him under the covers and sat on the bed with him until he would go to sleep. She really didn't have any choice about that; every time she shifted as if to get up, his eyes would pop open in alarm. So she leaned back against the headboard to wait him out. Her one advantage was having a molecule more stamina than he had.

As she quietly waited for him to go to sleep, Adair stroked the smooth black head and soft little cheeks. He was such a precious child, with such a tender heart—nothing he had inherited from Sandra, that was sure.

Adair inhaled, disquieted. What if he *had* really seen her? It was possible, as she also was tied in with the Warfield Group. If they already knew Fletcher was here, they could have sent her to distract him from what he was trying to accomplish. But did they know that his interest here was not financial?

Adair continued to stroke Daniel's head, gauging his relaxed, regular breathing. She sure needed to tell Fletcher about this. She also felt a strong curiosity to hear what was being said downstairs. So when she was certain that Daniel was asleep, she very slowly eased herself off the bed. To lessen the bounce of the mattress, she lowered herself to one knee first, then oh so gradually drew away from the bed.

She tiptoed to the door and looked back over her shoulder. He had not moved. Releasing her breath, she stepped out into the hall, leaving the bedroom door open a crack. Then she hurried down the stairs.

Adair heard the commotion before she came off the stairs. Lilith was crying, "How can you even think about doing this to me? How am I supposed to keep up this great big house without anybody to help me? After all those years of raising you without a father—! How selfish and ungrateful can you get?"

Peeking into the den, Adair saw Lilith and Cody arguing in front of the fireplace. Fletcher was standing quietly nearby. "But, Mom, he said he wants you to come, too!" Cody protested.

"Have you been talking to that man again? Was this Maynard's idea to turn you against me?" Lilith demanded in tears.

"No, Mom; this is Fletcher's idea. He wants both of us to go with him!" Cody insisted.

"Leave our home—everything we have—on what? His word that he'll take care of us?" Lilith asked as if Fletcher were not standing right there.

"Why not? The plant closing put you out of a job, and he just told you he wasn't going to reopen it. We got nothin' left here. We can't even meet this month's rent," Cody pointed out.

Lilith snapped, "Is all that supposed to make me feel better?"

Although Adair was as discreet as possible coming into the room, when Fletcher glanced over, he looked startled to see her. He came quickly to her side and took her arm, whispering, "What are you doing

99

here? Go upstairs with Daniel." Adair opened her mouth, taken aback by his abruptness.

He did not wait to hear any explanations. "Get upstairs with Daniel right now!" he hissed.

Stunned, Adair wheeled and left the room. She ran halfway up the stairs to the crook, where she stopped, taking in shaky breaths. Obviously, the argument unfolding in the den was none of her business. She didn't mind being told that (so she told herself), but what shook her was Fletcher's harsh tone. He had never spoken to her like that before, and it hurt.

Standing on the small landing, she nursed her bruised feelings. It hurt not to be the sole focus of Fletcher's attention anymore. That was the big reason she didn't want to leave Hawaii and come here, wasn't it? Helping these people meant that her own desires would just have to wait, which was not something a billionaire's wife was expected to tolerate.

Adair exhaled and tightened her lips. "Well. If that's what the *Boss* wants, then that's what we'll do," she said stoically, marching the rest of the way up the stairs.

Coming to the guest bedroom door, she softened in guilt. She had gone downstairs out of pure curiosity, hadn't she?—not to help or even learn, but just to skim some entertainment from Lilith's dilemma. "Shame on you," she scolded herself. "Stay out of the way and let Fletcher help them. He said it wouldn't be for long. Can't you put off ballet with Charity for a few days if it will mean changing someone's life? Sure you can. Grow up and stop—"

Having opened the door, she stopped dead. The bed was empty. Daniel was not in bed.

"Daniel," Adair said crossly, turning on the light to scan the room. Why couldn't he ever stay put? Not seeing him, she turned around to look into the open bathroom across the hall. It was empty as well.

"Daniel!" Adair called irritably, and his fear of Sandra sprang to mind.

"No. That's impossible," Adair whispered, coming into the room to check under the bed. "Daniel!" But he was not there, either.

Scrambling up, Adair began feverishly calculating the impossibility of Sandra's getting into this house, into a second-story bedroom, and taking him out from under them . . . while Adair was downstairs nosing around instead of up here with him, where she should have been.

"Daniel!" She ran from the room, and a movement at the dark end of the hall caught her eye. A door had just opened.

Adair ran to the door and stopped at the sight of the little body on the floor in the doorway. She had not seen him earlier because only his feet were visible in the hall. Her throat closed up in fear as she knelt over Daniel, touching his face.

For a few tense moments she sat with a hand on his head. As she regarded his rhythmic breathing and lightly closed eyes, her terror subsided. He held the blankie to his face in the relaxed grasp of sleep. He was asleep.

Adair sat beside him, unconsciously breathing in rhythm with him. He had never sleepwalked before. Even if he had walked out of the bedroom and down the hall in his sleep, opening this door, he would be standing, wouldn't he? Not lying here on the floor in the doorway. Unless . . . he was carried.

Adair stepped into the room and switched on the light. This was evidently Lilith's bedroom, being cluttered with feminine things. Keeping an eye on Daniel,

Adair briskly searched the room, the closet, the adjoining bathroom. No one was here, and the two windows were locked from the inside.

With slightly chattering teeth, Adair returned to Daniel and gently lifted him. He stirred, repositioning blankie, but did not waken. She carried him back to the bedroom and laid him on the bed, scooting him carefully under the covers. Then it suddenly dawned on her—Fletcher's tone in ordering her back up here was not angry, it was urgent. He knew one of them needed to stand watch over Daniel all the while they were here.

Her heartbeat was almost suspended while she concentrated every ounce of mental energy on this mystery. She could only conclude that there was something evil here, and Fletcher knew what it was.

She did not leave Daniel's side again that night, not even to go to the rest room. When Fletcher came in much later, he found her, fully clothed and sound asleep, curled up in bed beside their son. He got in bed without disturbing either of them.

✳

When Adair opened her eyes, the first thing she saw was Fletcher's head on the pillow beside her with Daniel's head lodged firmly against his neck, both of them still asleep. She raised up with a half smile, glancing at the pale morning light coming through the shuttered window.

Then she looked back down at Fletcher in his undershirt, his arm draped loosely over Daniel. A person wouldn't know to look at him how strong he was, but Adair never felt afraid when his arms were close by.

Groaning slightly, she dragged herself out of bed

to wash up in the bathroom across the hall. Oh, how she wanted to get out of this town! This morning, she didn't care about solving mysteries or doing good deeds; she just wanted to get the heck out. Maybe it wouldn't be too much longer. She consoled herself with a warm shower and thorough tooth-brushing.

When she came back into the bedroom Fletcher raised his head sleepily, rubbing the stubble on his face. Daniel was still comfortably glued in his side. "We were talking about how to get him to sleep in his own bed," Fletcher mumbled, shifting.

"No point in worrying about that here," she said with cheerful resignation, sitting on the bed as she toweled her hair. Lowering the towel, she related, "When I got back upstairs last night Daniel was on the hall floor, almost in Lilith's room. He was out like a light, and I don't think he had been sleepwalking. Fletcher . . . what's going on?"

He shrugged slightly, rubbing his neck. "He told me he saw Sandra yesterday," she added, watching him. "Is that possible?"

"Anything's possible," he said evasively.

"Do you think Sandra could be here?" she pressed.

He opened his mouth, then leaned his head back on the pillow and looked at her without replying. Adair began to feel irritated. "Fletcher, is Daniel in danger? At least tell me that!"

"He's not in danger," Fletcher said hastily.

"As long as one of us is with him," she added.

"Well, sure. We're his parents; we need to watch him wherever we are," he said.

Adair was not particularly happy with the way this conversation was progressing. She stood, shaking out the towel. "Can you tell me what happened with Lilith last night? Is she coming with us?"

"She's thinking about it," he said.

"Good. When are we leaving?" she asked eagerly.

"When I'm done," he murmured.

Adair sighed. He wasn't any easier to pin down now than he had ever been. "Fletcher, I'm scared. This place is evil. I want to go home," she said calmly.

He studied her. "You're not in danger because you're here with me. But if *you* feel like this place is evil, how do you think the people here feel? Can you stomach a little discomfort so we can fish a few of them out?"

She plopped back down on the bed, causing Daniel to open his eyes. "Fletcher—what is it about this place that they can't leave except with you? What is going on here?" she asked in rising anxiety.

Grunting, Fletcher sat up and repositioned drowsy Daniel in his side. He ran a hand through his mussed black hair, meanwhile glancing out through the broken slats in the shutters. "Fletcher Streiker, you're putting me off," Adair suddenly said in humorous disbelief.

"Me?" he said guiltily.

But then Cody appeared at the open bedroom door. The teen looked a little pale and haggard, and Adair couldn't help noticing he was wearing the same long undershirt and checked flannel shirt that he wore yesterday. "Uh, Fletcher, Daynell's here and I can't find Mom. She's not in her room."

"Okay, Cody; let me throw on some clothes and I'll be right down," Fletcher said, getting up.

"Right. I—think I may know where Mom might be. I'm gonna go check," Cody said before departing, his heavy boots clunking down the stairs.

"Ready for breakfast, Daniel?" Adair offered, bending to rummage in their suitcases for fresh clothes. This provided a good excuse to go downstairs, as she

104

wasn't about to get stuck up here again during another interesting conversation.

So the three of them dressed and ambled down the stairs. As Adair sat Daniel, blankie, and bunny at the kitchen table, she saw Daynell waiting in the den. There were only cold ashes in the fireplace this morning. Adair kept a discreet ear tuned toward the den while searching the cabinets for cereal. "I want *poi*," Daniel said in a grumpy, early-morning voice.

"Not possible, sweetheart," Adair said cheerfully, locating an oatmeal box. "Just pretend this is *poi*. Shh," she whispered, glancing toward Daynell and Fletcher in the other room.

"Good morning, Daynell," Fletcher was saying, his voice still low with sleep.

"Mr. Streiker," she nodded, stroking the arms of her fur coat. As she remained bundled up, it did not appear that she intended to stay for long. "I just came by to tell you that I did what you asked. I fired Powell," she said with a brave quiver.

"Okay," Fletcher said.

There was an uncertain pause. "So what did you want me to do now?" Daynell asked as if expecting the worst.

"Uh, just get him out of the store," Fletcher said.

"I fired him," Daynell repeated.

"Then he's out of the store," Fletcher repeated.

Daynell became flustered. "Who's supposed to help me with inventory, then?" she let slip.

Fletcher shifted, crossing his arms. "If you fired him, why is he helping you with inventory?"

"Well, he just—oh, he started crying and begging for another chance, and I told him I'd let him help me *without pay* if he'd *promise* to behave himself. He swore he would, and I knew that you were the type of person to give a person a second chance," Daynell pleaded.

Fletcher stared at her dully. "And how many second chances have you already given him?" he wondered.

She shook her head earnestly. "This time it's different. He knows you're serious and you won't put up with any foolishness."

"Daynell," Fletcher cleared his throat, "if Powell wants me to give him a second chance, then he's going to have to come *to me* for it—not go through you. You're going to have to step back out of the way, fire Powell, and *remove him from the store* like I told you to do."

Daynell's eyes flooded with tears. "Ohh! You're the hardest, meanest man I ever met in my life! I wish you'd never come here!" With a dramatic flourish, she rushed out of the front door, crying.

Adair watched from over the boiling water on the stove. Then she hastily dumped in the oatmeal flakes and began stirring. Fletcher came into the kitchen to sit heavily at the old wooden table. Daniel crawled over into his lap and curled up, unfurling blankie to find a good stiff corner. This he contentedly stuffed into his mouth while his daddy held him.

"Would you like some oatmeal?" Adair asked Fletcher.

"Sure," he said distantly.

"Now I must be asking the right questions," she quipped, adding another half cup to the pan.

"Adair, if . . . if we get separated and you get scared, go to the church—the one we stayed in night before last. Wait for me in that church," Fletcher said.

Adair quickly looked at him, but his expression was nothing more than thoughtful. "All right," she said mildly.

"Me, too. I get to go, too, if I get scared," Daniel volunteered.

Adair sat beside them. "Did you get a little scared last night?" she asked gently.

Daniel squirmed. "A little. You're not s'posed to leave me," he chided.

"I know." Adair nodded and got up to check the oatmeal.

About that time the front door opened and Cody banged in, shaking off snow and stamping his feet. "Fletch?" he called.

"In the kitchen," Fletcher said, scooting back from the table expectantly.

Cody came in and sat, tossing greasy brown hair back off his forehead. "Okay. I found Mom," he said, and paused.

"And?" Fletcher prompted.

"Uh, yeah, she was at the lodge with a bunch of other people. I heard a little on the phone yesterday—Tige Boston called this meeting of all the guys you were gonna buy out, and they're all at a meeting talking 'bout what to do. I just looked in the window," Cody said nervously. Fletcher merely nodded.

Adair turned off the heat under the oatmeal and went to the window to look out. The sun was a little brighter this morning, but there was just as much snow and ice blocking the roads as there had been yesterday. Yet all those people who insisted they couldn't get over here to meet with Fletcher were now meeting with each other behind his back.

That is when Adair realized she had been viewing the weather through the eyes of a southerner. Fletcher was correct in his assumption that these folks could make their way here if they really wanted to. These lifelong residents had adapted to getting around in the snow. It became an obstacle only when it suited them.

"Isn't Tige Boston the owner of Little Bangkok? Who was so anxious for you to buy that he kept lowering his asking price?" Adair asked, turning from the window.

"Yeah. Some people want an offer just for the pleasure of turning it down. I'll play that game—for a while," Fletcher said ominously.

"Was Sophie at this meeting?" Adair asked Cody.

"Uh, I don't remember. But Mom was, and Tige, Jerry, Gus, Powell, Mayor Halpin . . . there were others, but I just got a glance in and I don't remember who all." Cody got up to fetch a box of toaster pastries from the cabinet and pop two in the toaster. Adair meanwhile dished out servings of oatmeal with cinnamon and sugar for Fletcher, Daniel, and herself. When Daniel looked over to Cody's breakfast with greater interest, Cody tossed him a pastry hot out of the toaster. Daniel happily sat up on his knees and used the pastry to scoop up bites of oatmeal.

"So, what do you think they're going to do?" she asked Fletcher.

He shook his head, his eyes somewhat glazed. "It doesn't really matter what they do, collectively. They haven't got time."

Then we are leaving soon! Adair rejoiced inwardly. Although she noticed Fletcher's heaviness of spirit, she refused to let it infect her good mood.

So they ate breakfast and made small talk. Adair discovered that, contrary to the image he projected in the company of his friends, Cody was intelligent and impressionable, especially by Fletcher. The teenager talked to him freely about his frustration at school, his fear of not fitting in, his yearning for something more exciting than making trouble with Case (the biggest juvenile delinquent at the restaurant yesterday).

"And I look around at this town, and Go—I mean, gosh, it's so dead. So—closed up. Like a fishbowl, you know? I feel like we're just a bunch of fish swimming round and round in this tank, not going anywhere or doing anything," Cody complained. "So after Daryl left last year, I made up my mind that I was leaving, too."

This piqued Adair's interest, as Fletcher had said that nobody could leave without him. "Have you been here before?" she asked him.

Fletcher stirred. "Not in person. I called Daryl," he murmured in explanation, stirring the oatmeal thoughtfully.

"Didja? I had a feeling you had something to do with it," Cody said, then asked, "And how about ol' Webberley?" Fletcher nodded an affirmative.

"Gosh. I didn't think I'd ever get to see him again," Cody said softly. "He was a neat old guy—used to take me fishing and tell me stories when I was a little kid. We'd sit on the bank of the pond, and he'd tell me all about when he was a boy, catching snakes and swimming in the creek. He was the only guy I knew who seemed to think—I dunno, that it was good to be a boy. It was okay to have fun; there were fun things you could do that wouldn't get you in a pack of trouble, like the dumb stuff Case pulls. He taught me how to whittle reed whistles and press leaves. But he was lonely, you know? He always seemed kinda sad and lonely. . . .

"Then one day Webberley said he was going home; he was goin' to go swimming in the creek and catching tadpoles again. I thought he'd fallen off his rocker; he couldn't even walk without a cane. But the next day he was gone. Just upped and left everything behind—his clothes, his cane, his fishing pole. I never told anybody, but I cried for days. Then I got a letter from him telling me he'd made it; he was home, and he invited me to come go fishing with him. I asked Mom to take me, but she just kept putting me off, and I didn't hear from him again," Cody reflected, blinking.

"Surely he'll come back for a visit," Adair said brightly as she stood to gather empty bowls.

Fletcher looked up and Cody shook his head emphatically. "No way. Nobody who leaves ever comes back."

Adair paused, bowls in hand. "Not even to visit?"

"Not for thirty seconds. That's why Mom was so bent outta shape over me going. She knew she'd never see me again unless she came, too," Cody said.

Adair sat slowly at the table. "But . . . I read in the paper about people going on trips, and coming to visit—and you were on the phone to your dad, telling him to come."

"The town paper is controlled by the publication arm of the Warfield Group, Adair," Fletcher mentioned.

Cody added wryly, "I was kidding myself about Dad coming. He was telling me it wouldn't work, but I wasn't hearing him. Nobody who really leaves ever shows up here again. Now, there's some who *say* they left and came back, and there's some saying they're gonna leave any day now, but everybody here knows deep down that once you leave, you're gone. That's why they're all in a stew 'bout Fletch—they know he's here to take them away, and they're scared to go. Everybody hates it here, but they don't know what's out there. They're afraid they might not be able to cut it on the outside. So they just plod on. Not me. I'm outta here."

Adair stared at him, then looked at Fletcher. He

110

was watching her while Cody talked, studying her as if to ask, *Are you listening, Adair?*

For a moment she felt helplessly bewildered. What was she supposed to make of Cody's little speech? That he understood better than she why Fletcher had come?

As Cody got up from the table and headed into another room, the doorbell rang. He paused in the doorway to ask Adair, "Um, do you mind getting that? I gotta visit the john."

"Of course," she murmured, vaguely embarrassed. She went out of the kitchen to the television room en route to the front door.

Passing through the television room, she glanced down at a stack of paperbacks next to the recliner— evidently when Lilith wasn't watching trash, she liked to read it. Adair noted one book that had gotten knocked from the pile onto the floor. Just a glimpse of its black-and-purple cover sent a shock of recognition through her. Impulsively, she bent to pick up the book on her way to the door.

Opening the door, she saw Gus Gramble standing outside. "Is your husband here? I'd like to talk to him," Gus said gravely.

"Yes," Adair said, clearing her throat. She stepped back, almost bumping into Fletcher as he came up behind her.

"Gus," he nodded, "c'mon back while I put on a fire." Gus took off his logger's cap and followed him grimly into the den.

Behind them, Adair looked down at the paperback in her hand. This had to be one of the books what's-his-face was selling—one that Fletcher said ate souls like acid. Adair had read this book when she was about twelve. It was a novel about a beautiful, tragically

111

misunderstood teenager who killed herself. Adair had identified so completely with the misty-eyed Alexandra— they both had all the same problems—that she began to plan her own death just as Alexandra had done. It was impossible to forget the book's description of Alexandra in her white coffin, and the victory she scored over her stepmother by her last words, left in purple ink on pink stationery: "I never could please you."

What had spoiled Adair's plan was the actual suicide of a classmate a few weeks later. He had shot himself on the back porch of his house before his mother came home from work. It was anything but lovely: he had blown away half his head, leaving a horrifying sight for his mother to find when she went out to the patio looking for him. His friends were stunned and shaken, his stepfather racked with guilt.

Yet after all the drama of grief and goodbyes, it took only a few weeks for his classmates to put him behind them and go on with their lives. That's what caused Adair to abandon the plan, finally—when she saw how little difference it made to anyone except his family. And for them, it was hell on earth. Day in and day out they carried the horror of his suicide with them, and years later Adair heard that his mother could still close her eyes and see the gruesome remains of her precious child on the patio, dead by his own choice. At that time Adair's mother had told her, "If you ever hated me enough to do that to me, I wish you'd just shoot me instead."

That was when Adair had dug the long-forgotten book from its hiding place in her closet, taken it out to the woods behind their house, and burned it. Recognizing it as intrinsically evil, she did not want anyone else to be influenced by it as she was.

Adair stared at this book now, tempted to throw it

in the fireplace as soon as Fletcher got a good fire going. "I just might do that," she murmured, "but at least I need to compensate Lilith for it."

Opening the book to find a price, Adair stared down in mute terror at a name written in a familiar hand inside the front cover: "Adair Weiss."

I t was her very own handwriting—there was no question about it. There was even the little lily Adair had drawn after her name, symbolically indicating her intentions of following through with Alexandra's plan right down to the lilies in her folded hands.

Sick with consternation, Adair stumbled to the doorway of the den where Fletcher stood talking with Gus, the owner of the hardware store. She could not bring herself to interrupt them with something so bizarre and personal, so she had to stand there and listen, clutching the paperback.

Gus was telling Fletcher, "—and I've been elected spokesman of the group. Our first action will be to challenge you in court over the firing of Powell Rodgers."

"That's hardly necessary. If Daynell is unwilling to fire Powell, then I won't have anything to do with her business. She is officially back with Delightfully Yours. Now, would you say she's better off than with me?" Fletcher asked, leaning over for the fireplace shovel.

"In all probability, yes. We can hardly expect one outside owner to be better than another," Gus said tersely.

"But I'm not an outsider. I'm here. When was anyone from Delightfully Yours ever here to actually look at her situation in person?" Fletcher asked.

"That's not the point. You don't live here," Gus argued.

"Neither does your son," Fletcher observed.

Gus's face went red. "This has nothing to do with Joey," he said tightly.

"Doesn't it? Joey works for me," Fletcher replied.

"That's a lie!" Gus exclaimed.

"Check it out. Call him. When was the last time you talked with him? He lives in Alconquin now," Fletcher told him. Obviously, he had gotten the information he wanted from Yvonne some time last night.

With Gus knocked off balance, Fletcher went on the offensive. "So, what did you find out about me? Still haven't done your homework? If you haven't talked to Joey to see what kind of a boss I am, maybe you've talked to Cal Horton. He used to work at your store, didn't he? You fired him without cause and without notice. Well, he came to me, then, and I financed the start-up of his ski shop in Breckenridge. It's provided a nice little return for both of us—"

His blood pressure rising, Gus cut him off: "I ain't hearing no more of this, with you trying to turn everything back on me. All I came to tell you is that you're treadin' on thin ice, and you just better watch your step!" He jerked his hat back on his head as he turned to the door, bumping Adair on his way out.

116

She regained enough presence of mind to check on Daniel, crawling under the den coffee table in search of the cat. Then she took the paperback to Fletcher and placed it in his hands. "Look in the front cover," she whispered. Gus and his threats were trivial compared to this.

He glanced at her and opened it up. As he regarded the name written inside the front cover, she said, "This book used to be mine. I burned it." He looked up at her.

At that moment the front door opened and Lilith came in with another cold gust. "My. Whew! What a wind!" she said with exaggerated casualness to her guests.

Cody leaned on the den door frame. "Where ya been, Mom?" he asked with some bite in his voice.

"Oh, out visiting around. I saw Daynell. She wants you to know she's made up her mind to let Powell go as of today," she assured Fletcher. Without replying, he bent to resume cleaning out the fireplace ashes in preparation of building another fire. Cody eyed her angrily, then threw himself out the front door. Startled by his action, Lilith laughed, "Teenagers!"

Adair went up to her and showed her the book. "Lilith, where did you get this?"

"That? In the used-book section of the bookstore. It's one of the most popular teen books around, but Cody's just not into reading," she said ruefully, hanging her coat up on the hallway rack.

"Thank goodness," Adair said. She returned to Fletcher and took his arm imploringly. He straightened, lowering the fireplace shovel. "Fletcher, you have to tell me how this book got here. Am I going crazy?"

He leaned back. "No, you're not. The truth is . . . people who leave here don't come back—usually. But, you have been here before. The book belonged to you while you were here."

Adair braced the mantel to keep it from spinning. "I—don't remember even visiting here before. Ever."

"You were here," he maintained. "If you don't remember yet, pieces will start looking familiar to you soon."

Old Man Brunley's house—and the white dog— "But Fletcher," she pleaded, "I burned this book!"

"You thought you destroyed it, but you didn't," he said simply. Adair looked down at the book trembling between her fingers and suddenly wondered if she knew what was real anymore.

"Here. Let me do it," Fletcher said, taking the paperback. He tossed it into the fireplace ashes, where it sat unscathed for several seconds. "Lilith, Sophie has some books at her store I think both you and Cody would enjoy more. If you'll come on down with me this morning, I'll pick them up for you," he said.

Lilith glanced indecisively at the fireplace. She cared nothing for the book on the ashes—hadn't even read it—but it was a little disconcerting to have a guest throwing her property in the fire. "Those old books in the corner of her store?" she laughed derisively. "Goodness, I don't know anybody that's read them."

"I do. I know some people who left Beaconville after reading them," Fletcher said softly.

"In that case, I'm not interested," Lilith said sharply. The paperback in the fireplace suddenly burst into flames with a crack like gunfire. In seconds it too was ashes, and Fletcher resumed sweeping them up.

Lilith turned to Adair, who was staring into the ashes. "Well, have you come back to stay?" Lilith asked in friendly interest. "That *is* rare, for someone who left to come back—we hardly know of anyone who's done it. If you've come back, then I guess you belong here, don't you?"

"No!" Adair said in horror, head jerking up. "Fletcher, don't leave me here!" she cried, her eyes watering.

"I won't, Adair," he said firmly.

"Then let's leave today. Please, let's leave today," she pleaded, shaking.

"Soon, Adair," he whispered.

She sat on the hearth, blinking miserably, while Fletcher quietly finished sweeping the ashes into the ash bucket. "Goodness, all this carrying on, as if it were such a horrid place," Lilith murmured, offended. Shrugging, she began unwrapping the scarf from around her hair curlers as she climbed the stairs toward her bedroom.

Meanwhile, Daniel, sighing in boredom, gave up the search for Sphinx. He moseyed through the television room to press his nose against the front window. Then he turned from the fogged-up window and whined, "Mommy, I want to go build a snowman."

"He wants to go build a snowman." Fletcher nudged her, smiling. "Go wan. How many snowmen is he going to get to build in Hawaii?"

Adair glanced up disconcertedly. "You're right. I need to chill," she joked weakly. She steeled herself with the repeated reminder that Fletcher was apparently not shaken nor surprised by whatever bizarre things happened here. Getting up, she called to Daniel, "Okay, come put on your coat and gloves and we'll go out."

Daniel readily submitted to being bundled up, and Adair borrowed a few mufflers hanging on the hall rack for herself and him. Then they went out into the snow.

Even though the sun was no more visible today than yesterday, the clouds seemed not quite as dense, so that here and there snow crystals caught enough light to sparkle. It would have been pretty except there was so much of it, and it was so cold.

The front steps and walk had been more or less cleared almost to the street, but off in the yard the snow was several feet deep and undisturbed. When Daniel tried to climb up the snow bank to walk on it, the crusty snow gave way under his feet and hands. He tried to make a snowball, but the stuff was too powdery to hold together well. So he concentrated on blazing a new trail through the yard to the street.

While keeping an eye on him, Adair scanned up and down the street. She noted the layout of the block and the uniform appearance of the slightly run-down houses. She thought back to the area around the train station, the church, and motel. Then she shook her head firmly. Except for Old Man Brunley's house, none of it was familiar in the least. So what could Fletcher have meant?

She shivered. The cold was fierce, even when the air was still. It was the kind of piercing cold that settled in your bones and made them ache—the kind of cold you could tolerate for only so long before everything began to go numb. Daniel's nose and cheeks were already bright red.

Adair began to call him to go back inside when she noticed a lamppost in her peripheral vision that seemed out of place. Looking straight at it, she realized it wasn't a lamppost at all, but a man standing about sixty yards off, watching them. When he saw that he had been spotted, he began walking over to her.

Adair studied his stride and the graying blond hair on his bare head. He hunched his shoulders, steadying himself as he crossed an icy patch in the snow, and Adair felt the dull thud of recognition in her stomach. Daniel saw him and began to thrash through the snow to get back to her. But Adair held her ground while the man, smiling and nodding, approached.

"I heard you were staying here! Hello, sweetheart!" he greeted her.

"Hello, Daddy," she said calmly. Why was she not surprised to see her father, Carl, here? "Who told you we were here?" she asked. Her own opinion was that it had to be someone in the Warfield Group, as he was probably still tied in with them somehow. You didn't work for them once and then walk away.

"Oh, it's a small town. Word travels fast," he said amiably, peering at her through the tearing, cloudy eyes of an alcoholic. Adair thought him rather cheerful considering that the last time they saw each other, he had unsuccessfully tried to extort a large chunk of money from her. Daniel, remembering him, froze where he was while the snow hardened around him. But Adair felt nothing—no fear, no pity, no astonishment. This was just another bizarre coincidence in this bizarre little town. Right now, she was numb down to her toes. Yet in the back of her mind was the reassuring knowledge of Fletcher's presence just past this door.

Adair began plowing her way through the snow toward Daniel, enlarging the trail to where he was stuck. She asked over her shoulder, "How long have you been here?"

"Oh, a while," Carl answered hazily. It wasn't necessary for him to say what he wanted; Adair already knew: anything preceded by a dollar sign would do. If he couldn't get it one way, he'd try another.

As she reached Daniel and lifted him out of his hole, he fastened snow-crusted arms around her neck.

121

Turning to carry him back toward the house, she said casually, "Daddy, Fletcher thinks I've been here before. Did we ever come through here on a trip or anything?"

"Well now, I don't rightly remember," he said, squinting. Adair shook her head—wrong question. He'd be hard-pressed to remember much through the years of binges and hangovers.

"Come in. You must be frozen," she said, carrying Daniel up the steps to the door.

"That I am," Carl said, placing a shaky hand on the railing. "Um, your old man ain't here right now, is he?"

Adair glanced back as she opened the door. "Fletcher?" she laughed, deliberately evasive.

They paused in the small foyer to shake off coats and mufflers and hang them up. Adair nodded toward the glow of the fire visible from the den. "Go on in and warm up—I'll find us some hot cocoa."

Freed of his coat, Daniel darted into the den. Carl followed, chuckling, "If you can make that a Scotch, I'd appreciate that better." She said nothing, entering the kitchen to open a cabinet door and look for cocoa. But at the sudden silence from the den, she had to peek in.

Carl had found Fletcher standing by the crackling fire, holding Daniel. From his father's arms, the boy looked back over his shoulder in triumph at the mean old man who had scared him so. "Ahh," Carl stammered in unpleasant surprise.

"Hello, Carl. I understand you were wanting to see me," Fletcher said.

"See you?" Carl repeated blankly.

"Didn't you come to Honolulu looking for me?" Fletcher asked.

"No, that wasn't me. No sir," Carl said. The fact that he was lying was emblazoned across his face.

"Did you need money?" Fletcher asked.

Carl hesitated at this unexpected question. Then he opened his mouth and proceeded with the most amazing sob story Adair had ever heard. He told Fletcher about the associates who cheated him, the bureaucracy that strangled his business, the harass-ment of the Internal Revenue Service, and on and on.

Five minutes into the narrative, Adair stopped lis-tening to go make cocoa. Some of his complaints she had heard before and some actually had roots in fact, but the whole amounted to the most pernicious con-spiracy ever visited upon a hapless mortal. Fletcher listened without comment throughout the entire fif-teen-minute spiel.

When Adair came out with a tray of four steaming mugs, Carl quickly wound down: "So, seeing the kind of money you have to spread around, I didn't know but that you might want to do something for your little bride's old dad. I'm a proud man, and I don't accept charity, but if we could talk about a loan then I'd sure be appreciative," he said in all humbleness.

Fletcher set Daniel down on the hearth to drink his cocoa. Holding the warm mug with both hands, Daniel scooted right up to Fletcher's knee to keep a wary eye on the old sot. Carl sniffed his mug of cocoa; as it was unenhanced, he glanced at his daughter with a peeved look and rejected the drink. Adair handed another mug to Fletcher; when he took it, he caressed her fingers and smiled.

The contrast in their manner toward her summed up a vast portion of Adair's life: what her father had withheld Fletcher poured out. The attention and affec-tion Adair had yearned for but not received from her father, Fletcher provided. And Fletcher filled those empty places in her fragile heart so completely that

123

even when her father tried to tighten those old screws again, the buttressing within held up. She didn't feel a thing.

After taking a cautious sip of the steaming cocoa, Fletcher said, "Most people who come to me for help haven't got a prayer of paying back what I give them, so I don't talk much about loans. Just grants. This is great, Adair. Thanks."

"It's just instant," she murmured.

But Carl was speaking at the same time as she, and his voice dominated: "If that's the way you like it." He shrugged, indicating he himself liked that just fine.

"But of course, even grants require an auditing. Especially when someone comes back for seconds," Fletcher said.

"Excuse me?" Carl said.

"What did you do with the hundred thousand I already gave you?" Fletcher asked, taking another sip.

Carl looked flabbergasted. "Hundred thousand! When did you—you never gave me no hundred thousand!"

"I certainly did," Fletcher replied. He placed his cocoa mug on the mantel to rifle his pockets, locating a folded strip of paper, like adding-machine tape. Unfolding this paper to consult it, he told Carl, "On November eleven of last year, you received a check in the mail for exactly one hundred ten thousand dollars from the Bravora. That was one of my companies."

"That was settlement for the excruciating pain and suffering I received on their premises!" Carl shouted.

"We investigated your complaint and found it groundless. As a matter of fact, I saw photos of you two-stepping at Billy Bob's the evening after this 'debilitating' fall," Fletcher said. His mouth open to deliver an outburst, Carl froze. Fletcher continued, "I authorized the payment anyway, because you were destitute. So where did all that money go?"

His mouth hanging open, Carl's eyes shot around the room as if searching out excuses. "Well, I've had . . . expenses. I gave a large amount to charity, and I've had past-due taxes. My health has been poor lately, and doctor bills have just been eatin' me alive. Got a bum knee that needs surgery. Can't work at all for this blasted knee," he muttered.

"Uh-huh," Fletcher said drily, scanning the adding-machine tape. "I was curious as to how a person might spend an unearned windfall like this, so I kept tabs on you. Would you care to know where that money actually went?"

Carl looked apprehensive but curious, so Fletcher detailed from the tape: "The day you cashed the check, you dropped approximately two thousand renting a party boat on Lake Ray Hubbard, two thousand for food, and another five thousand for liquor. A few of your guests relieved you of seven thousand, and you had to pay another three thousand in damages. That's pretty good, Carl—nineteen thousand on one party."

"Dang, I musta had a good time," Carl said in admiration.

"Must have. The next day you bought an Acura NSX for seventy-five grand and squired a female friend around town to quite a few places—should I list them all out, or do you want the bottom line?" Fletcher asked.

"Just give me the total," Carl said, craning his neck to see the slip.

"Okay. You went through fifteen thousand that day," Fletcher said.

"On one gal? Just that one?" Carl demanded.

"Just on her," Fletcher confirmed.

"Who was that with me?" Carl asked, confounded.

"Uh, Lisa. No last name," Fletcher relayed from his paper.

"Lisa! That gold-digging tramp! She sure is pretty," Carl reflected. "How much did that leave me?"

"You were down to pocket change by then," Fletcher said. "Not enough to replace your car when you totaled it two days later. I believe it's still sitting in the body shop, with a past-due wrecker bill taped on the windshield."

"But I made a large contribution to Saint Bartholomew's," Carl said righteously.

"Actually, no. You signed a pledge for ten thousand, which you never paid. Since you claimed it against taxes due, I think that's what the IRS wanted to talk to you about," said Fletcher.

"They were hounding me so much, I had to get medication for nerves," Carl said with a sour face, holding his stomach.

Fletcher nodded, "Yes, you went to the doctor twice over the next week for ulcers and anemia. Your bills were partly covered by Medicaid, and the rest remains unpaid."

"Do you know how much he charged for fifteen minutes of his precious time?" Carl asked, outraged.

Fletcher raised a brow. "However much he charged, all he's seen from you is the twenty dollars Medicaid paid. Now, do you want to see where the last thousand went?"

"I get the picture," Carl said sullenly.

"You blew the whole hundred and ten I gave you in a matter of days with nothing to show for it. You proved yourself reckless, stupid, and dishonest. So why should

I give you any more?" Fletcher asked, sticking the paper back in his pocket to pick up the mug.

Beaten, Carl shrugged and looked at the floor. "I will, though," Fletcher added. Carl and Adair both looked at him in surprise.

"I'll give you a day-by-day allowance—just enough to make it through each day," Fletcher said. "Provided you go to work in my alcohol-treatment center in Dallas. You'll start as janitor. You'll live there, too."

Carl gaped at him with a lopsided, ironic smile. "Ah, thanks, pal. Tempting offer, but I think I'll pass on that." He swung toward the door, glancing coldly at Adair in that manner calculated to wound. She returned a level gaze.

"Carl!" Fletcher called, and he stopped with a hand on the front doorknob. "We're leaving on the next train that comes through town—the Morning Sun. When you hear that whistle, you better get on that train."

"Sure. Whatever you say," Carl nodded with grave pretense. Then he pulled his threadbare coat on around him and yanked open the door into the cold. Adair watched him go.

Slowly, she turned back to Fletcher. At first she did not know what to make of the expression on his face—the look was more than satisfaction, it was exuberance, zest—and all because he had shown Carl what a louse he was?

Fletcher's deep brown eyes shifted to her, and he grinned. He reached out for her hand to pull her as close as he could, considering Daniel was in between their knees. "Sometimes," Fletcher said, "all it takes is a good swift kick in the rear."

"Don't get your hopes up, Fletcher. I can't see him coming with us," she said cautiously.

He started to reply, but then raised his face as Lilith

127

came slowly around the corner from the stairs. Evidently, she had been eavesdropping on his conversation with Carl, and did not like what she had heard. "What's on your mind, Lilith?" Fletcher asked with the ease of confidence.

She twisted the bracelet on her wrist, looking from Fletcher to Adair to Daniel on the floor between them. "I think I'm sorry I invited you here. I don't understand what you're trying to do. It was fine—wonderful—when you were buying up the businesses downtown. I thought then that you cared about our town and wanted to help us. But now you're trying to get everyone to leave! You're breaking up families and good friends—you turned my own son against me! Why are you doing this to us?" Lilith cried in agitation.

"Because Beaconville was never meant to be your home, Lilith. You wound up here by default. I have in mind a much nicer place for you," Fletcher said softly.

"Beaconville is just fine!" Lilith bristled. "So we're not a big fancy metropolis like Dallas—we have everything we need, and with just a little work, and a little investment by someone who cared, this could be the best place on earth to live! I can't imagine wanting to leave!"

Fletcher nodded. "That's the problem—you've been imprisoned here for so long you can't imagine leaving. I've unlocked the door and all I'm trying to do is convince you to walk out."

"But it's not a prison! It's our home! And what you're suggesting is getting people all riled up. I have to tell you, I'm afraid. You're making people mad here!" Lilith exclaimed.

Fletcher agreed, "Yes, certain people are mad because I'm tearing down all the lies they've built around themselves for shelter. They're trying to take refuge in something that won't protect them at all! The truth is, Lilith, anybody who wants to survive has got to get out soon, because in a few days this whole town is going under."

"T he whole town going under!" Lilith repeated, shocked. "Why—why would you do this to us?"

"Hey, don't blame me." Fletcher held up his hands. "I'm just telling you what's going to happen so you can get out in time."

"If you hadn't come here, none of this would have happened!" Lilith cried.

"No, it still would have happened. The only difference is, everyone would be trapped with no way out," Fletcher said.

Lilith was peering at him, trying to decide what to believe, when the front door banged open. Cody, panting and flushed, ran in. "Mom! Fletch! The Country Attic's on fire!"

"Sophie's store!" Lilith gasped, staring at Fletcher.

"We'd better get out there," he said grimly. Then he paused, looking down at Daniel curled up on the floor.

The little man was already exhausted, but too keyed up by the tensions around him to think about a nap. Fletcher turned to Adair. "You and Daniel stay here. I'll be back soon."

Adair nodded in some dismay. Fletcher and Lilith threw on their coats and hats and left with Cody bounding before them. Then the house settled into quietness.

Adair inhaled soundlessly, looking down at Daniel on the floor. He turned large brown eyes up to her. "I want Mr. Fuster," he whined.

"You help me find him. C'mon," she said, bending to pick him up.

They located Fuster and blankie on a chair in the kitchen. She carried them all unresisting up the stairs to the guest bedroom, where Daniel gathered his friends to his face and burrowed down in the covers. "Don't leave me," he murmured.

"Don't worry," she said, stroking his smooth head. Being alone with him in Lilith's house made her whisper, for some reason—almost as if she did not wish to make their presence known.

Adair continued to stroke his head while his heavy eyelids sealed shut. It was early to be napping—not even noon yet—but the stress made for weighty hours. She wished she could find some escape in sleep herself, but didn't care to try without Fletcher right here. There were too many unknowns, too many oddities, too many impossibilities, as if the normal rules of reality had been suspended in this one little town. Fletcher knew what was going on—knew so thoroughly that he told them outright what was going to happen. Why wouldn't he answer her questions? It was clear that he wanted her to watch and listen, but when nothing made sense, what was she supposed to learn?

Wearily, Adair got up from the bed and went across

the hall to use the bathroom. She washed her hands and splashed water on her face. Doing all this took only forty seconds; then, knowing that she mustn't leave Daniel alone, she returned to the bedroom. When she looked into the room, what she saw caused her to freeze in the confusion of encountering the unheard-of. At first she could not move but only watch, as the sleeping Daniel was lifted from the bed and carried toward the door. He was clearly being lifted and carried. The dilemma to the senses rested in the fact that no one doing the carrying was visible. Confounded, Adair watched as Daniel floated toward the door feet first.

Then she snapped to and reached out to take hold of him. His slight weight rested in her arms without resistance, and she carried him back to bed. She laid him down, watching to see that he remained down, then she felt about in the air above him and around the bed. Her normal senses told her nothing was amiss, defying what she had just seen with her own eyes.

She sat over Daniel for the next hour, leaving his side only to open the bedroom door wider to be able to hear when Fletcher got back. Once she dozed off—she didn't know for how long—until her inner watchman woke her. She startled up, grabbing for Daniel, but he had not moved an inch.

Finally, she dimly heard the front door open and voices waft up from the den. Adair went to the top of the stairs and called down, "Fletcher! Fletcher, please come up here!"

In a moment he was trotting up the steps, blowing on his cold red hands. "Sophie's here—she's okay, but her shop and apartment are a total loss. It looks like arson," he commented.

"Fletcher." Adair grabbed his arm and dragged him

to the bedroom door, where they could look in on Daniel. "Fletcher." It took a moment for her to compose herself enough to talk. "I went to the bathroom," she whispered. "When I came back, Daniel was floating—just floating out of the room. I grabbed him and put him back in bed." Then she looked at him, pleading wordlessly for a shred of sense to keep herself together.

"Uh-huh," he said, glancing into the bedroom. "Well, we just need to keep our attention on him."

"Fletcher," she whimpered, "I can't go on, unless I understand more . . . you've got to help me understand."

He paused to choose his words carefully. "Adair, have you ever heard of the 'powers of the air'?" Her wide-eyed expression told him she hadn't. "Well, it's like . . . in certain places there are currents, kind of. Children are highly susceptible to them. These currents tend to separate people, to drive them apart and keep them apart. As long as our attention is on Daniel, he's all right. But when we stop thinking of him, it creates a vacuum for these currents to come in," he explained.

Adair protested fearfully, "But, then, when we sleep—"

"When you're asleep, I am watching over you both. But when you're awake, I'm relying on you to watch over Daniel. It's very taxing for me to keep up your end, too," he said, a little peeved.

"Taxing," she murmured. "How is it . . . taxing?"

"I'm, ah, expending a lot of energy keeping numerous currents at bay while we're here," he said slowly.

"Expending energy," she repeated in a monotone that signaled information overload. For several seconds she stared off into space, then focused on his face again. She reached up to touch him as if to reassure herself that he was flesh and blood. He took her hand and kissed her palm comfortingly. "Fletcher, what is this place? Where are we?" she asked in a whisper.

"This is not a place that you can pick out on a map," he said softly. "This is a state, Adair."

Her eyes glazed over again and he turned toward Daniel, who was stirring. Gathering bunny and blankie to his face, Daniel slid off the bed and came to his father without opening his eyes. Fletcher picked him up, and Daniel laid his head on the strong shoulder.

"Do they always wait till he's asleep?" she asked vaguely, but Fletcher understood the question.

"That's when he's most vulnerable. When he's awake, he can stop them with the slightest resistance. But he has to be alert to stop the drift. Some people—adults, too—get caught in the currents and are just too unaware to realize they're drifting out of control. Before long they get so far out that if they do wake up, they don't know where the heck they are. Some never wake up until they go over the falls," Fletcher said.

"Falls? What falls?" Adair asked quickly.

"All the currents drift downstream. You gotta swim against the current if you want to get to a safe place," Fletcher said. Adair stared at him.

"Let's go see how Sophie's doing," he suggested, hoisting Daniel. "The currents have been pretty bruising where she's swimming."

They went downstairs to the den, where poor Sophie sat slouched in front of the fire. Lilith put a hot toddy in her hands, and Cody stood in the doorway regarding her in dismay. Her gray hair was mussed; her clothes mismatched and rumpled. Having lost her spirited bearing, she now looked like a doddering old lady. "All my keepsakes and dolls," she said brokenly, "all that priceless old lace . . . and my books. My dear old books that were such a comfort to me. . . ."

Fletcher sat down with her. "I have better copies of the books you lost. And the other things don't matter. I'll make you so comfortable that you'll never remember losing anything," he promised quietly.

Sophie looked up, smoothing back gray strands with a shaky hand. "I received an anonymous call this morning—he said I had better call off my deal with you or I'd have nothing to sell. They did this to me because of you," she said tremulously.

"Probably," Fletcher said.

"Then . . ." Sophie looked around distractedly, "then what reason do I have to stay here? Why do I live in a place where people do this to each other? I don't want to live here anymore! I don't want to stay here one more day!" Adair could almost see her waking up, kicking out of the currents' flow.

Fletcher grinned. "Stick with me, Sophie, and I'll take you to more beautiful shops than you ever imagined. I'll put you in charge of the most exquisite laces, the finest handmade porcelain dolls, and the rarest engraved books in the world."

Sophie gazed at him with the wonderment of a child. "Why . . . why would you do that for me?"

"Because I know that the only people competent to handle valuable things are the people who truly appreciate them," he replied.

Sophie looked stunned, then jumped up from the hearth. The "little old lady" disappeared in a crackle of excitement, and there stood a purposeful woman. "When do we leave? Let's go!"

"Yeah!" Cody said, catching on. "What've you got for me to do, Fletch?"

Fletcher smiled. "Cody, I'm gonna teach you to fly."

"Fly?" Cody said in dazed disbelief. Visualizing the possibility, a giddy smile broke on his face and he agreed, "Fly! Yeah! Wow!" Then he looked at his mother, deliberately holding herself aloof from the others' excitement. "What about Mom, Fletch? What can you do for her?" Cody asked.

"Lilith, if you come with me," Fletcher promised, "I'll find you someone to love. Someone who needs you desperately."

Lilith blinked at him, and again Adair saw a person emerging from the crushing weight of currents that were smothering the life from her. "How can you do that?" she asked timidly.

"I know a lot of people who have a lot of needs. And I know someone who aches to have your arms around him," Fletcher said.

Lilith's face flushed in either embarrassment or hope. Seeing that her secret desires had been exposed, she lowered her red face and excused herself to the kitchen.

Crestfallen at her lack of enthusiasm, Cody looked to Fletcher, who nodded. "We'll keep after her," he said quietly. Cody looked back to the kitchen.

When Adair realized that Lilith was working on lunch for them all, she left Daniel with Fletcher and went in the kitchen to help her. Pulling deli meats and condiments from the refrigerator, Lilith barely looked over. "I wasn't expecting guests. I just don't know what we're going to eat," she grumbled. Then she stared at the package of shaved ham in her hand. "Where did this come from? I don't remember buying this."

In growing bemusement she brought out oranges and fresh lettuce, handing them to Adair to put out on the butcher-block table. "Cody! Did you go to the grocery store?" Lilith called, but Cody did not hear her.

In a place where children floated out of beds and objects from her past appeared, Adair did not question sudden provisions at the household hosting Fletcher. She found plates and napkins while Lilith put on a fresh pot of tea, then they called the others to come in for sandwiches.

While they were all standing around the table making sandwiches (and Daniel was swiping olives), the doorbell rang. Several faces looked toward the door in alarm, but Cody manfully put down his plate and said, "I'll get it."

The group in the kitchen was quiet while Cody went to the door. They could not tell who was there, but after hearing what the visitor said Cody replied, "He's here. Come on in." Adair glanced at Fletcher, who turned in interest.

A preteen girl bundled up to her eyes shyly followed Cody into the kitchen. "That's Fletcher," Cody said, pointing. "This is Andi Cain."

"Hello, Andi," Fletcher smiled. With his Hawaiian tan and worker's build, he made a good impression on almost any girl subject to infatuation.

"Hello," she murmured, glancing at the other people standing around.

"Let me take your coat, Andi," Lilith said, taking a stab at hospitality.

The girl lowered her hood, shaking her dark blonde hair. "I can't stay but a second. Oh—didja hear about Case and Boone?" she asked Cody casually. "The sheriff picked 'em up for hittin' the drugstore Wednesday night—they got 'bout eighty dollars, some pills and stuff. The sheriff let Boone go with his folks, but Case's still locked up."

"Uh. Bummer," Cody muttered.

Andi nodded. Her blue eyes rested on Sophie a

moment, then she looked back at Fletcher. "Care for a sandwich?" he asked.

"Nuh-uh," Andi declined, loosening the muffler from around her neck.

"Then what can I do for you?" he smiled.

It was a simple, honest question that emboldened her to blurt, "I hear you're invitin' people to leave Beaconville with you. What I want to know is, who all can come?"

"Anybody who wants to," Fletcher said.

"I want to go, but I don't have any money for a ticket. I don't have anything," she said flatly. She looked so certain of being turned down that Adair suddenly wanted to put her arms around her.

"I don't need anything even if you had it," Fletcher replied with a slight twinkle. "I've already purchased all the seats on the train. What I do need are people who will help me get other people out of here before the town's reduced to ashes."

"How do you know everything's going to get burned up?" she asked suspiciously.

"It's already started," he replied, nodding to Sophie.

Andi fixed him with a preteen's idea of a hard gaze. "Some people say you started that fire yourself, to make her leave."

"That's a lie!" Cody blurted.

Fletcher glanced at him. "That's not the way I operate, Andi. I won't force anybody out, not even to save your own lives."

"What do you care about us?" she asked bluntly.

A quick spasm of pain crossed Fletcher's face. "It hurts to see what you're doing to yourselves, especially since I know how well off you could be. If you saw a puppy caught in a wolf trap, wouldn't you try to get it out?"

Andi looked down to the floor, murmuring, "Nobody knows how horrible my life is."

"I know you cry yourself to sleep most nights. I don't want you to cry anymore," he said softly.

As Andi raised her face, the beating of her heart was almost audible to Adair. "When are you leaving?" the girl asked.

"When the next train comes through. When you hear that whistle, you need to get right on that train," Fletcher said.

"When will that be?" Andi asked.

"I don't know. I don't have the schedule. I just know it's going to be soon," Fletcher said.

"What if it's in the middle of the night and I don't hear the whistle? What if I get on the wrong train?" Andi asked fearfully.

"There's only one train coming, Andi—the Morning Sun. And don't worry, you'll hear it. Everyone who's listening for it will hear it," Fletcher assured her.

Andi thought about it, then nodded. "Okay. If you say so."

"I say so. Remember, you gotta get to the station as soon as you hear the whistle. Don't dawdle," Fletcher reiterated.

"Okay," she said with greater resolve. "'Bye. 'Bye, Cody," she added, raising her hood.

Cody told her goodbye and Fletcher said, "See you at the station."

Andi left, the front door banging behind her. Those in the kitchen were silent a moment, then Lilith wondered, "How could you know that she cries herself to sleep at nights?"

Fletcher pretended not to see Daniel swipe a potato chip from his plate. "Lilith, I . . . know a whole lot about the people here. I've done a lot of research on you because I knew I'd have just one shot at this town, and I wanted to make it good."

"What, do you have people spying on us?" Lilith asked stiffly, echoing a question Adair had once asked.

"Who needs people to spy? The walls and the woodwork tell me everything I could stand to know about you," he said, his voice tinged with tiredness. "There are more eyes and ears around you than you could ever guess." So saying, he picked up his sandwich and took a large bite. The thought prompted an apprehensive expression to cross Lilith's face that was mirrored in Adair's.

She was not so perturbed that Fletcher knew every less-than-flattering detail about her—she could have guessed as much—but that there was so much around them that defied normal explanations. Powers of the air? Walls that had ears and eyes? Was it just this way in Beaconville, or was Beaconville just the setting for the exposure of these hidden agents?

Glancing around at their dazed faces, Fletcher explained, "People who moved away from here came to me talking a mile a minute." The others then relaxed, but when she caught his lingering glance, Adair was more inclined to believe his first explanation.

Following lunch, Sophie began to pace through the small first-floor rooms restlessly. "Maybe everything wasn't destroyed. Maybe I can salvage something," she mused.

"Nothing there is worth salvaging, Sophie," Fletcher objected.

"But there might be *something*," she fretted, apparently forgetting his promise to provide her with far superior replacements. "I have to go see," she said decisively.

"It won't help," Fletcher warned.

"I have to. I have to see if there isn't anything left," she insisted, going for her coat on the hallway rack.

Fletcher sighed, glancing back at Adair. "Well, I can't let you go alone—it's too far a walk. Let me go with you." He also got his hat and coat off the rack.

"I'm going, too!" Cody jumped up, at the ready.

"Okay." Fletcher turned to Adair. "We'll try to get back as soon as we can. Just—stay alert."

"You can count on it," she said drily, and he grinned halfheartedly.

Those three departed into a day that had grown meaner and more blustery since the morning. Adair had no wish at all to go out with them. But when she turned back to find Daniel loitering in pathetic boredom, she did wish for something to occupy him.

Daniel himself solved the problem by finding the marbles Adair had taken away from him yesterday. This discovery prompted him to search out more marbles. Despite the fact that he wouldn't go upstairs without Adair (and Cody's room, site of a treasure trove, was upstairs), Daniel still found a sufficient amount of marbles to divide them up and start a war between them.

While Lilith busied herself with laundry, Adair divided her attention between Daniel in the den and the front windows in the television room. She stared out at the pickets of the fence rising up from the snow like a row of tombstones. And as she looked, ideas rose like ghosts from what she thought was dead ground. A comprehensible picture of this town and her place in it began to take shape in front of her. She began to understand.

Lilith passed behind her with an armload of towels for the downstairs bath, and Adair said, "He can do everything he says, you know."

Lilith paused. "I'm sure," she replied.

"You invited him here to change things! Why won't you let him?" Adair asked, turning.

"I certainly didn't expect him to take away everything we have!" Lilith exclaimed.

"But that's just so he can give you better things!" Adair insisted.

"How do I know that?" Lilith demanded.

"Because that's what he did for me," Adair said softly, turning back to the window. "I remember this place now. I didn't at first, because once you leave you tend to put it out of your mind—to pretend it doesn't exist anymore. But that's not good. You always need to remember exactly what it's like here, so you won't be tempted to come back."

"I don't believe you really know anything about us," Lilith snapped.

Adair smiled vaguely, still staring at the snowdrifts. "Oh yes, I do. Sandra is here, and Carl is here, and Old Man Brunley. And though I haven't seen him, I know of someone else who is here—a man by the name of Darren Loggia. Do you know him?"

"No! Not at all! Of course not! Why in the world would you think I knew anything about anyone like that?" Lilith arduously denied, her face pale.

"Then he is here, too," Adair nodded slowly. "Lilith, this place is a graveyard, and everyone here is dead unless you let Fletcher get you out."

"That's a fine threat!" Lilith huffed, still white.

"I'm not threatening you; I'm telling you the truth! You're *already* dead, six feet under! You have *got* to let Fletcher break open the casket while he's here. Once he leaves it will be too late!" Adair pleaded.

"I have never heard such nonsense in my life!" Lilith declared hysterically, and the doorbell rang.

Adair checked on Daniel, who was rolling marbles down a crack in the wood floor one at a time, then apprehensively followed Lilith to the door.

She let in someone all bundled up; when he had loosened his muffler and removed his hat, Adair saw it to be Gus Gramble. As he squinted at her with watery eyes she fleetingly wondered, *Why does he keep coming back here?*

To bolster her courage, Adair drew on what knowledge she had of this strange place. "Fletcher is not here right now," she said, and Lilith faded behind her.

"I'm aware of that," Gus replied. "I came to see you. Things are liable to get ugly real soon, and we all agree we got no quarrel with you and the little boy. So Jerry brought his truck to take you on out to the hotel in Catawa."

Adair looked out to where the pickup sat idling in the street, its exhaust pipe steaming. "No, thank you," she said wryly.

He shifted impatiently. "I'm not in a good humor, honey. Just get the boy and go get in."

"Not on your life," she retorted. "Besides, Fletcher said it isn't possible to leave without him, and the only way to get in or out is by train."

He came toward her abruptly, eyes glinting. "You come now," he breathed. Hostility settled on him like an aura, and she felt the bullying push to fear. At that moment she recognized the rush of the current trying to sweep her away.

Adair laughed in his face. "You can't make me go anywhere! You're just a shadow—a ghost! Now leave me alone!"

At this blunt refusal Gus's face changed abruptly, and he looked confused. "I just thought . . . we'd try to help you out. Since Streiker wants people to leave, we're volunteering to help him get anybody out who wants to go."

"Thanks, but no thanks," she said, eyeing him. "We're leaving by train, like he said."

Gus shook his head sadly. "Honey, I hate to tell you this, but this weather's done a number on them tracks. There ain't no telling when the next train'll get through."

"I'll let Fletcher worry about that," she said cautiously, as the fearful suspicion reared up that someone here might make sure the tracks were sufficiently damaged to prevent their leaving.

"Whatever you say," he shrugged dubiously. "I'd just hate to see you stuck here for long, with all the bad feelings your husband's stirring up."

"Thanks for your concern," she said, expressionless. With a small jerk of his head, he pulled his hat back down over his ears and trudged out to Jerry's truck.

Lilith shut the door behind him pensively. She said nothing at first, but then noted, "The bridge to Catawa's been out since November. Gus should oughta know that. But you're going to offend people, calling them ghosts. *I* am not a ghost."

"I'm sorry, Lilith," Adair sighed. "I'm trying to find words for something I've never seen before." At that point she remembered a curious statement Daniel had made.

Adair went into the den where he was playing with the marbles. She got down on her knees, then sprawled on her belly as he was. He pushed a handful of marbles toward her. "You can be these guys," he offered.

"Thanks." Adair rolled the marbles between her hands. "Daniel, what did you mean when you said nobody here was real?"

"They're not," he said in typical four-year-old abstruseness.

"Well—is Daddy real?" Adair asked.

"Of course, silly." He rolled his eyes.

"Am I real?" she asked.

He stunned her by saying, "Yeah, when Daddy gets you out of here."

❧ 9 ❧

"I'll be real when Daddy gets me out of here?" Adair repeated weakly, and Daniel nodded. "Hasn't Mommy always been real?" she asked.

He looked up with a pensive expression. "Will you love me when I have a different face?"

"I'll always love you, Daniel," she whispered. He went back to playing, going so far as to appropriate the marbles he had given her. Adair, shaken, got up from the floor. She went back to the front room to look out on the dismal whiteness.

Fletcher said this wasn't a place you could find on a map. He called it a state. Has some part of me been here all my life, then? Am I dead inside? A ghost? It was horrifying to think that all the while she had been going to school, studying ballet, working at the bank, her innermost self existed in a shantytown with bogeymen. *That means I am no different from them*, she thought bleakly.

But then there was Fletcher. Somehow, he was her escape route as surely as he was theirs.

Soon thereafter the front door banged open and three huddled forms hurried in. Cody, being too macho to dress warmly, flashed through the den to stand just about on top of the fireplace. And poor Sophie took off her coat and hung it up with an air of despair. As the last one in, Fletcher stood in the doorway to knock the snow off his black hat. "Did you find anything left?" Adair asked, holding her arms against the cold.

Fletcher moved in and shut the door, shaking his head. "It had been picked over before we got there. Somebody had to be literally walking on coals to pilfer the place. But neither of the adjoining businesses was damaged," he observed.

"Mrs. Potters was supposed to have been at work, but she wasn't. She was at home. I called her from the five-and-dime, to tell her about the fire. And she did not even care. She already had another job elsewhere! She did not care because it was not her life that went up in smoke, though I took care of her like my own daughter," Sophie rambled, heartbroken.

"I'm sorry," Adair said. She wanted to remind Sophie what Fletcher had promised to do for her, but to say anything of the kind while Sophie was still grieving her loss didn't seem right. Then it occurred to Adair that if the people here weren't real, then their possessions were certainly less than nothing.

"Sophie, they just saved you the trouble of deciding what to pack. You can't take more than a suitcase on the train," Fletcher told her. "Besides, when you see what I've got in Dallas, you're not going to want any of the stuff you brought, anyway."

As Sophie considered this, Adair thought how fortunate it was, in a strange way, that her shop burned.

All those lovely things that she cherished might have given her second thoughts about leaving town with Fletcher. But now that they were ashes, she had nothing to lose. "Very well," Sophie murmured. "If you don't mind, Lilith"—she turned around looking for Lilith, who had sat down in front of the television set for one of her favorite soap operas—"if you don't mind, I'd like to lie down," Sophie requested.

"You can use my bed upstairs," Lilith said, then settled in the comfy old recliner as the show's theme song began to play.

"How about some more of that cocoa, Adair?" Fletcher asked with an affectionate hand at her back.

"Sure." She smiled in sympathy at his blue lips. Sometimes he seemed so invincible it was hard to remember that he could be uncomfortable, too. While Adair filled the teakettle and turned on the stove, he went in the den to check on Daniel. Dropping to his knees to get on Daniel's level, Fletcher showed him how to shoot marbles. Suddenly the marble war was forgotten as Daniel concentrated on learning to flick them properly. Adair glanced in the den, smiling at the two black heads huddled in all seriousness over technique.

Fletcher got up to let him practice by himself, and wandered over to Adair's side as she waited for the water to boil. He seemed restless, impatient. From the kitchen, he looked at Lilith staring with vacuous eyes at the television. Taking a chair from the kitchen table, he carried it to the television room, placed it beside her recliner, and sat next to her. "Wake up, Lilith," he said. Maybe he was joking, maybe not.

"Shh," she admonished. "It's about to start."

"When you get tired of living off of other people's daydreams, let me know," he said.

149

She ignored him. He persisted, "C'mon, Lilith, you wrote me because you wanted something better in exchange for your time. Something . . . more immediate. More exciting," he suggested, leaning closer to her.

"I enjoy it. Please be quiet," she requested.

"It's not as much fun as what you could be doing," he said in her ear. Adair glanced over at his seductive tone.

Lilith laughed ironically. "What, laundry?"

He lowered himself to one knee beside her chair. "Imagine yourself with someone who knows you're there—who feels your absence when you're not. Imagine him looking at you when you speak and listening to what you say. Imagine sharing your deepest secrets with someone who understands." His voice was low and gravelly with persuasion. Adair stared. How did he know so unerringly what each of them wanted most? And who was he talking about? Surely not himself!

At any other time Lilith might have listened to him, but right now she was locked up in an electronic box. Ironically, she hadn't even heard him. "In a minute," she said absently.

That was the currents' trap—*just a minute; not right now. Lie back down; you've got plenty of time.* So the minutes allotted her slip quietly by until they're all gone, and the joys she could have experienced remain buried under wasted hours.

"Lilith, listen to me," he said urgently.

"I'm happy with things as they are," she snapped back. As the show began, she blocked out everything else but the screen in front of her.

Fletcher stood up, considering how to get her attention. Watching, Adair forgot all about the water on the stove until the teakettle whistled a reminder to turn off the heat.

A movement outside the front window caught Fletcher's eye. He looked outside, then quickly turned his back to the window so that he was in between it and Lilith, still seated before the television.

There was a sudden crash and thud as a rock sailed through the window and hit Fletcher squarely in the back. He fell to his knees, grunting, as a second rock broke the window in another place and landed in the television screen. It sparked and crackled, then went blank. Outside, a four-wheel-drive spun off on the snowy street.

Adair ran to Fletcher's side, exclaiming, "Are you hurt?" After having decided these people were illusions, she was horrified to find that they could do real damage, especially to Fletcher.

"Uhh, not much," he groaned, straightening his back.

Lilith, livid, had sprung up to shake the television set, pound it, and cry. "Ohh!" She wheeled on Fletcher. "Look what you've done! It's ruined, and we don't have another! Oh, I wish to goodness I'd never written you! Go away and take Cody if you have to, but just leave me alone!"

Adair turned on Lilith with an angry retort, but Fletcher cut her off, instructing both of them curtly, "Go get your coats." The cold air pouring in through the shattered window was making them all shiver. Lilith, suddenly abashed at her outburst, didn't argue with him. Meanwhile he stepped to the foot of the stairs to shout, "Sophie! Come down now! Sophie!"

"What?—Coming!" They heard her call from upstairs. Cody looked in from the den and Daniel raised up.

"Everyone get your coats," Fletcher directed them with such stern eyes that they scurried to comply.

151

Adair immediately began bundling up Daniel, who tried to sneak a few marbles into his coat pockets. She caught him and emptied them, tossing the marbles onto the couch. "Are we going somewhere?" Lilith asked meekly, a little frightened by now. Cody got himself a heavier coat from the hall closet, as well as one for his mother.

"It's time to take a little tour. We're going to the outskirts of town," Fletcher said grimly.

"No," Lilith paled. "It's—it's so far—and we can't take the car—"

"That's what you've been saying ever since we got here. Now we're gonna find out. Cody, get the keys," Fletcher instructed.

Cody looked interested as he rifled his mother's purse. "Mom always said there was nothing out past Beaconville. What are we going to see?"

"We're going to take a look at what you'll be left with if you stay here," Fletcher said. "Then we'll see how much you want to stay."

Sophie, appearing in the front room, observed, "So there is something out there, after all. Everyone in town says there's not, but some of my little books say differently." She slowly put on her old woolen coat.

Lilith looked terrified. "No. I won't go with you. I'm staying here."

"C'mon, Mom, you might as well go. The TV's busted and you'll freeze your duff off if you sit here," Cody coaxed, forcing her coat on her. Besides which, it was obvious that Fletcher was poised to carry her out kicking and screaming if necessary.

With Lilith babbling pointless refusals, the six of them wrapped up and went out the front door to the detached garage. Fletcher, Cody, and Adair quickly shoveled enough snow from the driveway to get the door up (Adair using a gardening spade and Daniel assisting with a hand shovel). The cold engine of Lilith's ten-year-old sedan was loath to turn over, but Cody patiently turned the key, pumped the accelerator, and muttered the proper invocations until it roared up. He backed it out into the driveway, where they all piled in. Cody begged to drive but Fletcher took the wheel. With him in front were Daniel and Adair; Cody, Lilith, and Sophie warmed each other in the back.

With a glance in the rear-view mirror, Fletcher put the car in gear and backed out of the driveway into the street, sliding over the neighbor's mailbox. "Oops." He then looked over his shoulder instead.

Waving to the house with the downed mailbox, Cody cackled, "Have a nice day, Miller!" The car tires crunched the snow as they fishtailed slightly down the street. "Cool," Cody grinned. Lilith was ghastly pale.

Fletcher drove straight down the street (relatively speaking) away from downtown. When they came to a dead end, he merely slid around to the next street that led out. Many of the houses they passed had lights on or smoke coming from the chimneys, but no one else was trying to go anywhere right now. Adair held Daniel down in his seat belt while he kept trying to get up on his knees to see out.

Fletcher took them in this direction until they had shortly passed the last residential area of Beaconville. Then, they were driving down a winding, narrow country road all but invisible but for the barbed-wire fences that marked the bordering fields. They could see nothing but empty stretches of snow. "See? There's nothing out here. Take us home," Lilith said desperately. Without replying, Fletcher kept driving.

Some minutes later there was an abrupt change in the landscape. The snow disappeared and the sun came out. The dirt road ahead became visible. Grass and trees appeared in the fields along the roadway. Fletcher turned the car's heater off, then all of a sudden they were elbowing each other in taking off their coats.

Not even Adair thought to question this meteorological turnabout. She did notice something curious about the sun, however—though bright, it was not like the sun in Dallas or Hawaii; it had a slightly off-color cast, as if someone had made a slight miscalculation mixing the paints. Cody was making a halfhearted joke about getting a tan when the sight ahead hushed him as well.

They were approaching a huge, ultramodern office complex, constructed with mirrored glass panels that reflected the sunlight with blinding brilliance. A five-level parking garage near the main entrance of the complex was jammed with cars. It was such a sleek edifice that it impressed even a jaded Dallasite such as Adair.

Fletcher parked in the outer regions of the landscaped front lot and five silent, gaping passengers got out of the car with him. The outside temperature was somewhere in the seventies; the blue sky lightly dotted with clouds. But Adair vaguely noted that the clouds also had a contrived appearance—they were too round, too fluffy.

Fletcher led the group at a brisk stride through the parking lot. They passed so many gleaming, expensive cars that Adair was wondering if they hadn't arrived at the Galleria by mistake. Entering through the front glass doors of the complex, which opened to them automatically, they filed into a spacious, opulent lobby. Beyond the vast floor tiled in onyx, glass interior walls gave view to an atrium. Everything about it was unquestionably splendid, top-of-the-line. A large receptionist's desk sat at the far end of the lobby. Something was missing, but Adair was too overwhelmed to pinpoint it at this time.

"We don't have an appointment," Lilith blurted.

"I don't need an appointment," Fletcher said drily.

"Is this one of your buildings?" Adair asked him.

"No," he said, and his voice seemed to send a shudder through the lobby. Lowering his voice, he said, "This is the international headquarters of the Warfield Group."

Adair was too stunned to respond at first. Then she recalled, "I thought you said—they were out of New York City."

"They have a large base of operations there, but *this* is their primary facility," he said, remembering to keep his voice quiet.

"Wow. It wouldn't be so bad to have a suite or two on the fiftieth floor," Cody noted.

Fletcher glanced at him wryly. "Don't bet on it." He then reached over to a granite pillar and lightly swept his hand over it. The mere touch of his fingers gouged out chunks of granite like butter.

They all stared. "You lift weights?" quipped Cody, his voice cracking.

Fletcher smiled. "You try it. Daniel, touch something."

Intrigued, Daniel went over to a three-foot bronze ash stand and attempted to pick it up. It crumbled in his little hands like sand. He then pushed against the wall behind it, and the force of his hands drove deep holes in the polished stone. A wave of his arms opened a cavern in the wall. "Okay, enough. You're going to bring down the building around us," Fletcher said, restraining him.

Cody then reached out to a corner of the wall and took the edge of it off with the flat of his hand as if it were modeling clay. They all touched something and found it everywhere pliable. Adair could not even feel the granite that collapsed under her fingers.

"It's—it's as if there's nothing really there. What *is* this?" Adair asked, perplexed.

"A deception," Fletcher said, shaking his head. "Empty camouflage."

"Hey! How come we don't just drop through the floor?" Cody wondered.

"Because I am holding you up," Fletcher replied. "By the way, you couldn't poke holes in this place if I weren't here with you. If you came here without me, it would shut up on you like a steel trap." Respecting this, they quit exploring and huddled a little closer to him.

Suddenly Adair realized what was amiss. "Where is everyone? There are all those cars outside—where are the people?" There was no sign of anyone in the building besides themselves.

Fletcher turned to stride through the lobby, his companions following closely. "They ran to hide when they saw us coming," he replied.

Cody laughed. "Boo!" he shouted down a nearby corridor.

Fletcher glanced over, amused. "Just remember that it's me being with you that makes you so 'bad,' pal," he reminded Cody.

"Hey, I'm with you all the way, Boss," Cody said.

"Then come this way," Fletcher nodded. In trying to open a locked side door he inadvertently tore it from the wall, leaving an eight-foot crater with ripped wiring and wallpaper dangling from the exposed edges. "Whoops," he said. Cody couldn't resist knocking out another three-foot chunk with his hip.

This brought them to the outside of the complex, where they quickly covered their faces. Out here, a stench—an acrid, burning odor—pervaded the air. Behind the gleaming facade of the building, the ground was littered with the most disgusting refuse Adair had ever seen. As Fletcher led them gingerly around scattered piles, she was afraid to look more closely to see what exactly they were picking their way through. Daniel scrambled up into Fletcher's arms, and Lilith seemed about ready to faint. Adair glanced back at the building they had just exited. From this angle, she saw nothing but decrepit ruins.

Fletcher led them single file through the dump and up a short hill. "This," he said, looking down from the crest of the hill into the valley below, "is the dead zone of Beaconville—where it all comes to rest." His companions looked down in wordless astonishment.

On first glance it appeared to be a valley, but a closer look revealed it to be more a series of pits, like a mining quarry. The ones closest to them were the shallowest; they got progressively deeper farther away until the farthest pits were lost to the eye. Each pit appeared to be a world unto itself, totally separate and distinct from other pits a few feet away.

Here were the people, at least—or what was left of them. Adair found a curious capacity of vision here: whatever pit she focused on, she saw clearly without ever leaving the hilltop. None of Fletcher's group dared go a step closer to the chaos beneath them. They merely looked on.

In one pit close by, Adair saw a distinguished-looking man giving a serious scientific speech at a podium—or attempting to, at least. For his audience, an equally distinguished group of men and women, greeted everything he said with jeers and heckling. It was the loudest, rudest audience Adair had ever seen, especially for such an educated group. And their comments seemed to be personally directed toward the sweating, discomfited speaker.

As he tried to make an important point, one audience member stood up and shouted, "You ought to go back to the Stone Age where your methodology came from, Harper!" The rest of the audience applauded.

The speaker wiped his brow and said, "I apologize for making that unfortunate remark concerning your work, Dr. Barnes, but if you'll kindly listen—"

A woman shouted, "You can't be a *serious* researcher when you sleep with every lab tech around!" Hoots and lewd comments from the audience followed.

Speaker Harper wilted. "Dr. Reynolds, I truly regret that anyone took that offhand comment seriously. Heaven knows I certainly never believed you—"

"Hey, Harper! Tell us how you came by those numbers in your statistical analysis of the Scofield project!" another man shouted.

Wiping his brow, the speaker began to stammer, "It was late, and I was tired—you must understand the deadline I was under—yes, yes, I borrowed your data, Pete, but—"

The jeers attending this lame explanation were quickly hushed as one more audience member, a gray-headed man in a frayed lab coat, stood. Solemnly, he intoned, "Dr. Harper, your experiments are worthy of a third-grade science project. Your thirty years in the field have produced nothing of value on a scientific or humanitarian level."

An outburst of applause followed this appraisal, and Dr. Harper pleaded unheard, "The reporter provoked me into saying that! How could I know you would read that and then kill yourself? I didn't know, Gib!"

He seemed to be getting nowhere, so Adair turned her attention from that depressing scenario to another a little farther away. She saw a man walking down a dark sidewalk, his tense face coated with perspiration. He walked stiffly, unwillingly, watching a doorway ahead all the while. Suddenly two men sprang from the doorway and proceeded to beat him senseless, one with a bat and the other with a brick. When he was beaten to unconsciousness, they rifled his pockets and congratulated each other, whooping. Then they darted back into the doorway.

The victim came to, slowly picked himself up, and began stiffly walking on down the sidewalk. There was another doorway up ahead that he watched warily. Suddenly two men sprang from that doorway, and Adair witnessed the same brutal beating and robbery all over again. When it was over and they disappeared, he got up again, groaning, to continue walking down the sidewalk. He had gone only a few paces before being set on again.

Adair turned away, not wishing to watch any more of this. Curiously, she felt little sympathy for the hapless man doomed to walk the endless sidewalk. She had noticed that both his assailants were identical to him—they could have been triplets except for shades of difference in their ages. From this, Adair intuitively deduced that they were the same man at different stages of his existence—what he was then, and what he is now.

Adair focused on a pit yet farther off. But this next one was not as comprehensible as the first two. A woman was spirited through several scenes one after another: first she ran screaming through a creaky old castle where blood spurted from the walls while floors tipped down into poisonous quagmires; then she fell into a pit of vampires who clawed over each other to get to her veins; then she was trapped in a narrow room where razor-sharp tendrils exploded randomly from the floor to sever her hand or her foot. Running maimed through passageways that seemed to promise escape, she found herself trapped in a maze of endless gore.

Disgusted and confused, Adair turned to Fletcher: "What's going on with her? I don't understand."

Fletcher looked where Adair pointed and said, "She's a novelist—her particular genre is horror. Novelists get to live in the worlds they created."

Adair winced. "I don't see why they'd want to."

"What they want has nothing to do with it," Fletcher replied coolly.

"Glad I'm not a novelist," she muttered.

"So you don't write down your imaginings. What are they like, Adair?" Fletcher asked softly. Shutting her mouth, she looked back at the pit. Then she noticed that this pit bordered several others in the far reaches of the valley. She was frustrated in trying to look on these; as soon as she focused on one to make sense of it, a fog formed before it, obscuring it. She saw only enough to baffle her.

In one far pit there was a group of naked people in erotic play. They were chaining each other with heavy shackles into rough iron tram cars that sat on a track leading into a cave. Although they seemed totally unaware of the chains and iron seats, they still managed to fasten themselves in beyond release. Then the tram cars began moving, and disappeared into the hole like a roller-coaster ride. Adair heard screams and moans echoing up the track, then the fog rose.

In a neighboring pit Adair saw an extremely muscular man reach down and greedily pluck up some pathetic little being scrambling to get away from him. He swallowed the poor thing whole, making disgusting digestive noises, then spat up the remains. Incredibly, the remains seemed to still possess life as they scurried away from him, seeking burial. Then the fog rose again.

"What . . . ?" She turned with intensity to Fletcher standing beside her. "The fog comes up, and I don't understand what happens to the people in those two pits," she complained incoherently.

"The end result of lust is a little too strong for you to see," he said ruefully.

Adair then turned in concern to Daniel, lest he be frightened by such sights. But Daniel, holding on to Fletcher's leg, looked around in such apparent boredom that Adair asked, "What do you see down there, Daniel?"

"Just some people trying to play with a bunch of broken old toys. Can we go back and tear up the building some more?" he asked hopefully, looking up his father's leg.

Fletcher smiled down at him. "In a minute."

Adair looked at Cody, who was squirming. "Why does he keep chasing girls when his face is all rotted off?" he muttered. Then it dawned on her that they were all seeing different things.

"Fletcher, this . . . is this really Beaconville?" Adair asked faintly, and the others looked over.

"This is Beaconville near its core. Where Lilith and Cody and Sophie live, near downtown, is actually on the fringes. The bad news is, the core is expanding. If you choose to stay in Beaconville, Lilith, you will be engulfed by them," he said, nodding down to the valley. "All the restraints and the sanity of normal life will be peeled away. All you will have left is what you only wanted to bury." Lilith looked sick to her stomach. "What a terrible fate, to end up like that," Adair mused.

Fletcher shook his head. "That's not even the end of it. That's just *near* the core—there's the core." He pointed out to the farthest pit, where they saw a seething red mass bubbling up, momentarily threatening to overflow into neighboring pits. Steaming little trickles were already visible coming over its sides. That, and not the debris, was plainly the source of the stench. "That will be the end of anyone determined to stay in Beaconville," Fletcher nodded.

"Looks kinda nasty," Cody muttered.

"It's fatal. It will kill them," Fletcher said plainly.

"Screaming jalapeños, let's get out of here!" exclaimed Cody.

The others started scrambling down the other side of the hill, but Fletcher balked. "Well, I don't know; you said you wanted to stay," he baited Lilith.

"Stay, nothing! Get me out of here!" she snapped.

Fletcher smiled. "Follow me." He began leading them back through the illusory facade of the building.

Adair looked back to the far pit, where larger streams of red overran its boundaries. "Fletcher . . . is Darren there?" she asked fearfully.

He glanced at her. "Yes."

"I didn't see him," she said.

"Some things are not for your eyes," he repeated.

"But"—she was still groping for understanding—"if you came to get people out, can't you get him out? Or anyone else down there?"

"I can only drag them out if they're willing to go. Knowing what you know about Darren, do you think he'd let me?" Fletcher asked.

"Not a chance," she said grimly. "But surely, some

of those others—"

"I've already been down there once, and that's enough. Those you saw still here wouldn't come with me. But I've had a few successes. For instance, I worked your dad, Carl, out of there," Fletcher noted.

"Carl!" she exclaimed, and he nodded with some satisfaction.

A dismal thought sprang to mind, and she stopped in her tracks. "Oh, Fletcher—are my mother and step-father there?"

"Dana and Dale used to live in Beaconville a long time ago—so long ago that they don't remember it. I wish they would, because sometimes they act as if they still live here," he said pensively. Seeing her worried face, he assured her, "But they don't. They're safe."

"And my dad, Carl?" she asked.

"If he comes to the train, he'll be fine," Fletcher said.

"But what if he doesn't come?" Adair cried. Fletcher just looked at her.

They went back through the building, which seemed to be minutely quaking. Apparently the others felt it; Sophie exclaimed, "What's that?"

"Ah, it's all coming down shortly. Better get on out," Fletcher said, ushering them to the front door. The automatic eye failed to open the door. So Fletcher walked right through it, shattering the whole front entryway.

"This is great," Cody snorted, strutting through a sparkling shower of glass.

When they reached the car Fletcher noted, "Better get your coats back on."

Though sweating, they did, and climbed into their seats. Fletcher started up the car and headed back the way they came. In moments they saw the winter landscape ahead; in another minute it was upon them. Adair twisted in the seat to look out the back window— the fabricated springtime was no longer even visible. Winter prevailed once again as they reentered Beaconville's residential area.

It was fortunate that no one else had ventured onto the road because Fletcher slid all over it. "Why people even keep cars in climates like this beats me. They oughta just use snowmobiles," he muttered, fishtailing through a corner yard.

"See? Told you, Mom!" Cody exclaimed from the back seat.

"Shut up," she muttered, too shaken to be polite.

"Oh no," Adair breathed, looking ahead toward Lilith's house. There was a group of men out front who had evidently just rung the doorbell. Adair recognized Gus Gramble and Jerry Hayworth; the others, whom she did not know, were Tige Boston, Mayor Halpin, and the local sheriff. Their vehicles sat at the curb.

The carload was quiet as Fletcher slid into Lilith's driveway. While they got out of the car, the men made their way over on the icy sidewalk. "Mr. Streiker," the mayor called from ten feet away, "Mr. Streiker, ah, we don't want any trouble. We're a peaceful community and we just don't cotton to outsiders coming in stirring folks up. We've come to ask you to leave town right away. If you don't, we're prepared to arrest you for disturbing the peace."

"I can't leave until the train comes through," Fletcher pointed out. "All the roads around town are impassable."

"Not so," the mayor shook his head under his golf cap. His ears looked painfully pink, but he was too vain to wear earmuffs. "We've heard that Catawa has cleared the stretch between our towns. You can make it that far today. Sheriff Guftasson will even drive you in his squad car."

These reasonable men believed it to be a reasonable offer, but Fletcher looked at them askance. "And my wife and son? Do you propose I leave them here or cart them with me?"

"Whatever you choose. If it were me, I'd certainly want my family with me," the mayor said with a nod to Adair.

"And what if the road isn't clear? Will you turn around and bring us back here?" Fletcher asked. Something about his tone told Adair he was just debating for the exercise. He had no intention of leaving yet.

"We have it on good authority that the road is clear," the mayor repeated earnestly.

Fletcher smiled. "You are certainly the most brazen liar I've seen in a while. And a coldblooded son of a snake who'd strand a woman and child in subzero weather rather than let one person out from under your thumb. Darren will be proud."

Mayor Halpin's face flushed red to match his ears. "Sheriff, you may take him into custody," he ordered.

⇥ 10 ⇤

A dair almost lost her composure to see Fletcher handcuffed and prodded through the snow to the squad car. Daniel started crying, "Daddy! Where're they taking my daddy?"

"Wait—please, we need him—we're here alone—" Adair pleaded to deaf ears. Fletcher looked back at her with intensely meaningful eyes. She got the clear impression that he wanted her to remember something. She was supposed to do something. But she was too panicky to remember for the life of her what that was. So she and Daniel, Lilith, Cody, and Sophie watched in dismay as Fletcher was placed in the squad car and driven out of sight.

Their objective accomplished, the other men turned to leave as well. "Wait," Cody demanded suddenly. "Our window was smashed. You guys gotta find out who knocked out our front window," he insisted, pointing to the damage.

Mayor Halpin hardly glanced at the broken panes. "Probably one of your friends, boy," he uttered over his shoulder as they climbed in a second car. Tense and silent, the group watched the town officials depart.

Once they were gone, Sophie was the first to shake out of paralysis, snapping, "It won't do us any good to stand out here and freeze to death." She went on up to the front door and the others miserably followed her.

It was just about as cold inside the house as out, because of the ventilated front window. Cody found some boards in the garage that they wrapped with bedsheets for insulation before nailing them up over the broken panes. Lilith put on some canned stew while Sophie rekindled the fire.

When the window was boarded up, the fire started, and the stew heated, they gathered in the den to eat in front of the fireplace. Still, they had not taken off their coats. Lilith's cat Sphinx came in mewing, seeking comfort on Lilith's lap. Daniel was too distressed to pay any attention to the cat as he hung on Adair whining softly, "Where did they take my daddy?"

"They—they took him to the sheriff's office for a little while," Adair said, trying to comfort him. "He'll get things straightened out and get back to us. Don't worry."

"He certainly didn't help matters, calling the mayor a liar and a snake," Lilith noted, shooting a peeved look toward the dead television in the next room.

"So? He is one. He's both," Cody said defiantly. "Fletch was just telling it straight."

"Well, that certainly stoked the fires, and I'll thank you not to use that tone with me, young man!" Lilith said irately.

"He did, didn't he?" Sophie murmured, eyes on the fire. She looked at Adair. "Did it seem to you that he deliberately provoked them?"

Adair could hardly bring herself to consider the question. Deliberately get himself hauled off to jail, leaving her and Daniel defenseless in this horrible place? How could he do such a thing? "I don't know. I don't know what to think," Adair moaned.

"It was almost as if he had a preset plan," Sophie mused.

This observation should have jarred Adair's memory, but she was still too unnerved to think clearly. "If he did, he didn't tell me what that was," she said tightly.

Daniel crawled up in her lap. "I'm scared," he whimpered. Adair looked around, then spotted Mr. Fuster at the foot of the stairs. She got up and carried Daniel over to where the bunny lay, picked it up, and nestled it under his chin. "Here."

Daniel withdrew the bunny and threw it back down to the floor, complaining, "It's no good without Daddy." This alarmed Adair as much as anything yet, and she wondered, *Who is going to watch over us tonight?*

※

A fresh cold front blew in that evening. Cody and Adair sealed up gaps around the boarded windows with duct tape, and taped up towels over that, but the wind still knifed its way through all obstacles to chill them to the bone. The house's ancient heater gave out under the strain, so no one went upstairs to sleep. They all remained huddled under coats and blankets in front of the den fireplace. Daniel forgave Mr. Fuster enough to cuddle him and blankie under Adair's blanket. They didn't talk much, listening to the wind whistle in through the broken windows.

Adair glanced at Sophie several times, whose face was pinched with pain. "Sophie, are you all right?"

Adair asked, concerned.

Sophie tried to shrug, but sighed instead. "My old bones don't like the cold—it makes them ache so. Oh, I'm ready to live someplace that isn't so cold!"

"You'd like Dallas, then. It can get pretty chilly, but never for very long. We'll have an ice storm one day and then seventy degrees and sunshine the next," Adair smiled. "Oh, and Hawaii is even better! It never gets very cold, except up around the craters. If you want rain you just go to one side of an island; if you want sunshine you go to the other. And oh, the beaches! They're like something out of a dream. The black sand beaches will leave you speechless."

"Would Fletcher take us to Hawaii?" Lilith asked shyly.

"I'm sure he would. Everyone who knows him winds up there sooner or later," Adair said.

"That's where we live," Daniel said, wishing to make a contribution to the grown-up conversation.

Adair nodded, gazing into the fire as she recalled Hawaiian sunlight dancing down through palm fronds. Having spent so much time in that sunshine is what enabled her to detect the counterfeit sunshine around the Warfield Group headquarters. She bet Daniel had noticed the difference, too, but the others never said a word about it. She decided they had not seen enough real sunshine to recognize what was fake.

"I'll miss some of the guys here," Cody muttered. "I kinda wish . . . I dunno, I wish I had said more to Case and Boone about coming, too."

"Case?" Lilith snorted. "That juvenile delinquent would sooner rot in those pits than come with us!"

"Listen to you!" Cody exclaimed ironically. "Fletch had to drag your tail out—"

Sophie interrupted, "You may be right, Cody; but

you mustn't speak to your mother that way. Fletcher didn't." Cody dropped his head and nodded.

He got up a short while later to bring in more logs from the garage. Bundling five or six of them down beside the fireplace, he grunted, "This is all the wood we had left in the garage."

"That's all?" Lilith said, startled.

"Yeah. Zeb Miller's got a great fire going, though," Cody observed ironically.

Lilith looked bitter. "I knew I should have gotten that lock fixed. You just can't trust anyone anymore."

"Tomorrow we either get the furnace fixed or start chopping up furniture," Cody added, dropping a log on the fire amidst a shower of sparks. The comment stirred something buried in Adair's memory, but she still felt too paralyzed to think.

One by one they dropped off to sleep—all but Adair. For one thing, she was too keyed up; for another, there was the wind outside. It was a malevolent wind, rocking the trees and battering the shutters. There was no snow coming down at present—just that wind. To Adair, growing paranoid, it seemed as if the wind were circling the house, looking for a way in.

She gripped sleeping Daniel in her arms, thinking about currents. Something outside the den window caught her eye, and she quickly looked. By the time she had focused on the window, whatever it was had gone. She wasn't even sure anything had been there to begin with.

A loud bang, bang, banging startled her, and she looked again to the window. It sounded as if something were banging along the outside of the house, from the rear to the front, searching for weak spots. Adair's heart began pounding in her ribs.

At this, the worst possible time, she thought about

171

the scenes they had witnessed in the pits behind the Warfield headquarters. When that nasty red mass began to overflow the surrounding pits, what would the people there do? Stay and drown? Or would it force them out ahead as it coursed toward the outer reaches of Beaconville? If it forced them out, would they come this way . . . looking for shelter?

The pounding of her pulse made her inner ears throb. "Fletcher," she whispered, her eyes watering. "Fletcher, I'm so frightened. I don't know what to do."

Something compelled her to look toward the window again. There, on the outside, was the shadowy image of Darren's face peering in. Adair choked back a scream, and the image faded back into the wind.

She jumped to her feet, startling Daniel awake. "We have to get out of here!" she shouted without realizing it.

The others woke in alarm, peering at her in the dull glow of the dying fire. "What?" "Why do we have to leave?" "For Pete's sake, where're we gonna *go*?"

Adair caught her breath. "Now I remember! The church! He told me that if we got separated and I got frightened, to go to the church!"

Now her companions stared at each other. "Excuse me; are you crazy?" Cody asked. "Look outside!"

Adair shook her head resolutely. "It would have been easier had we gone earlier, but I didn't remember until just now. This house is just not sufficient shelter, and we have to get to someplace that is. Everyone double up on coats." Her calm, deliberate manner persuaded the others to do it. Lilith looked down at Sphinx, then gathered her up and tucked her inside her coat as if she were contraband.

Daniel transferred Mr. Fuster from one hand to another so Adair could put his coat and gloves on him.

"Will Daddy be there?" he asked anxiously.

"Probably not when we get there, but that's where he'll come look for us," she said confidently. This encouraged the rest of them that maybe she was not crazy after all.

When they were ready to leave, Adair shakily unlocked the front door. She breathed, "Fletcher, think of us," then opened the door into the wind.

It tore the door from her grasp and slammed it back into the outside wall. They filed out quickly, Adair carrying Daniel. The wind whipped gleefully around them as they thrashed their way through the snow to the car in the driveway. They bundled in, Cody inserting himself behind the wheel. "Turn on the heater," Lilith urged.

"Chill, Mom; I gotta get it started," he said, turning the key. The only thing that happened was a row of red lights on the dash lighting up. The starter did not so much as whimper.

"Uh-oh. We're dead," Cody said. Daniel began crying.

"Hush, darling," Adair said to one, then asked the other, "Is there any way to get it started?"

"Not unless we can find somebody with a live battery to give us a jump start," Cody said.

"Nobody's going to get their car out in this weather to give us a jump start to the church," Lilith said flatly.

Adair looked down the desolate street, the one with Old Man Brunley's house. "Okay, then. We walk," she said, opening the car door.

A chorus of protests rose. "Gimme a break!" Cody wailed.

Sophie asked quietly, "Adair, why is this so important?"

"Remember what Fletcher said, about the core

spilling out? It's happening now. I don't want to get caught in that, do you?" Adair said, shivering emphatically.

The others thought about that. "The church?" Lilith asked as if considering how to get there.

"Yes, the one by the motel. Do you know which one I mean?" Adair asked.

"There's only one church here," Lilith said vaguely. "But it's quite a ways. . . ."

"I know shortcuts," Cody countered. "We can do it."

They fell out of the car into single file as Cody led them slipping and sliding across the icy street. Behind him was Adair carrying Daniel and his friends, then Sophie, then Lilith holding Sphinx under her coat. From the street Cody plunged into the virgin snow on a neighbor's lawn, and they crossed between two houses.

The wind met them head-on with such force that it knocked Sophie clear off her feet. Lilith struggled to lift her with one hand, calling ahead to Cody and Adair. The rush was so loud that he never heard her, but Adair looked back.

"Cody!" Lilith was shouting. "Help Sophie!"

Adair called up to Cody, and they stopped to regroup. Cody laid Sophie's arm across his shoulders and resumed the lead. Tears of pain wet the muffler under her eyes, but she never said a word.

They pushed on, crossing through two yards until they turned into an alley. Here there were fenceposts they could grab at regular intervals to keep them on their feet; otherwise, they would have all wound up face down on frozen mud. The wind blasted through the alley as if it were a wind tunnel. *As bad as it is*, Adair fleetingly considered, *at least it's dry. If it was snowing, there's no way we could get there.*

They staggered down the alley for what seemed like

174

miles. Adair's face, hands, and feet went numb, and Daniel hung as dead weight on her. The wind caused tears to pour from her eyes and then freeze on her lashes. Blinking ahead at Cody lugging Sophie, Adair earnestly hoped that he knew where he was going.

A moment later Lilith just collapsed. Adair heard the faint plop, turned back, and saw her slumped at a fencepost. "Cody! Wait a minute!" Adair shouted. He looked back over Sophie, and Adair trudged to Lilith's side. "Lilith! Get up!" Adair ordered.

"I can't," she moaned, and her voice was almost lost in the wind. "You all go on. I can't make it."

Adair shifted Daniel to one arm. With the other she grabbed hold of Lilith's coat and pulled hard. "You have to come! You have to! Fletcher can't help us if we don't get where we're supposed to be! You come now, Lilith! I mean it!" Desperate and nearly blind, Adair screamed at her.

In response they heard Sphinx's plaintive meow, still tucked (or trapped) under Lilith's coat. Daniel raised his little face from Adair's shoulder to beg, "You gotta bring the kitty cat."

The gentle reminder did what brute force could not do. Groaning, Lilith let Adair pull her to her feet, and they staggered on up the alley. With the additional burden of mature Lilith on her arm, the remainder of Adair's strength ebbed quickly. As she fought the icy wind carrying Daniel and lugging Lilith, the black warning of imminent collapse began blocking out the sight of Cody and Sophie ahead.

At that moment she spotted the garish neon lights of the Best By Far Motel. Adair's sight cleared and she uttered a weak cry of relief, as the church was right next door.

In another moment they were scrambling up the

icy front steps of the church. Cody released Sophie to grasp the ornate iron handle of one door and yank. As before, it was locked.

He turned to Adair and yelled, "How are we supposed to get in?"

Adair swallowed a weary sob. "Go to the side door!" she blurted, knowing that in the two days since they were here, it would have been repaired, probably reinforced. If they couldn't get it open. . . .

They stumbled to the side of the church, painted by the motel's flashing lights. Adair put a hand out to feel for the knob, and the door swung open under her touch.

Astonished, they quickly crowded into the small office. Adair found the light switch, flicked it on, and they stood there blinking.

When Adair's eyes had adjusted to the light, she reached for the wall thermostat and turned on the heater. They all held their breath, listening in wonder as the furnace beneath them roared up. In a few minutes, warm air began ascending from the floor vents.

"Oh!" Lilith sat down next to the floor grate, crying in relief. Sphinx wobbled out from under her coat and shook herself.Cody turned to brace the door shut with a chair. "It's been kicked in," he noted, running a hand over the split framing.

"Fletcher did that, the first night we were here, so that we could get in," Adair said, trembling. "I thought it would have been repaired by now. . . ." She turned to the desk and saw the cash just where Fletcher had left it.

"Nobody has taken the money!" she said in amazement. "Hasn't anybody been here since Tuesday?"

The group looked at each other a little guiltily. "I don't know anybody who comes to church," Lilith admitted.

"Well—what about the minister?" Adair asked.

They all looked blank, then Sophie said weakly, "There was someone, some time ago, who I recall took it upon himself to refurbish the place and open it up, but then he left town. . . . It seems that almost everyone who made the effort to come here wound up leaving Beaconville."

"Oh." Adair inhaled, reaching out frozen hands to feel the precious warmth of the vents. "Well." She rubbed her hands, looking around. "Let's go to the sanctuary, where there's room to lie down." Having been here before, she acted as guide.

They filed past the kitchen into the carpeted sanctuary and turned on the lights. Adair looked over in gratitude at the window of Jesus at the door. For the first time, she took note of the other three windows: they depicted Jesus carrying a lamb on His shoulders, Jesus on the cross, and Jesus on a white horse. Before she had much chance to contemplate what they meant, she was distracted by Daniel throwing himself atop the floor grate. She promptly lifted him off, and in a few minutes they were all comfortably settled beside a stream of warm air.

"Well, I have to admit this is a sight better than my house," Lilith said. "But now I'm hungry."

"I want some grape juice," Daniel said, bouncing up.

"I'll have a beer, please," Cody requested, raising a finger.

Adair shot him a look. "There's nothing but grape juice and crackers, but I'll bring it," she said, getting up on stiff legs. She went to the little kitchen area, thinking that grape juice and crackers would be just fine. Now that they were where they should be, she felt safe for the first time since Fletcher had been taken to jail.

She turned on the light in the kitchen and looked

177

around. Not knowing where Fletcher had found the juice and crackers, she went over to the refrigerator and opened it. And almost dropped her jaw.

It was stocked with newly bought groceries, hastily thrown in. Fruit was still in plastic produce bags. There was milk and lunch meats and cheese and soft drinks. Adair picked up a grocery receipt lying atop the cheese. On the back side was scrawled in Fletcher's handwriting, "Good girl!"

"When did he do this?" she exclaimed, and then remembered the hours yesterday when she and Daniel were napping at the motel. "Fletcher!" she said, smiling.

She took out the milk carton to place it on the counter and there saw more groceries—bread, chips, rolls—even cat food and kitty litter. "How did you know that Lilith would bring her? Or that she would even come herself?" she said wonderingly.

The only thing to do now was call the others into the kitchen, so they could help themselves. Adair triumphantly appeared at the door of the sanctuary and said, "Okay, everybody! To the kitchen! Fletcher expected us to come and went shopping for us!" There followed a general dash to the kitchen.

Adair paused after the others left, seeing Sophie still sitting by the floor grate. "Don't you want something to eat?" Adair asked, coming over to her.

Sophie smiled up at her tightly. "I'm afraid my old knees just won't let me get up right now."

"I'll bring you a plate," Adair said, then began trying to list out everything in the kitchen: "He bought some wheat rolls, and blueberry muffins, and apples—"

"Whatever you bring me, I'll eat," Sophie said. "But I'd love to try the muffins."

"Sure." Adair smiled, then went back to the kitchen worrying about Sophie's knees.

"Where did all this come from?—fruit, and milk?" mused Lilith.

"Fletcher went to the store!" Adair repeated, opening the bag of muffins while Cody raided the chips.

"But with the weather, the stores haven't gotten any sweet milk or fruit in for weeks! Deliveries are never very reliable, but lately nobody's had any fresh produce to sell! Where did all this come from?" Lilith asked, perplexed.

Adair looked at the generic, old-fashioned cash register receipt, numbly shaking her head. "Remind me to ask him," she murmured.

No one else was much perturbed over the source of the goodies as they ate themselves stuporous off of Communion plates. Then they gathered around two of the sanctuary floor grates to sleep. Adair, cuddling Daniel, was again the last one awake, but now it was just to listen for a moment. She could barely hear the wind outside. She knew it was raging, but this old church was so solid and tight that the wind couldn't find any cracks big enough to blow in with much force. Adair drowsily wondered who in the world had managed to build a church in this awful place, then she shut her eyes and breathed, "Thank you, Fletcher," before falling asleep.

✳

In the morning Adair was gradually roused by a faint knocking. Opening her eyes, she looked up at the window of Jesus at the door. Then she sat upright, staring at the window while listening to the knocking.

"There's somebody at the door," Daniel said sleepily, and Adair looked toward the front doors of the church, which opened into the back of the sanctuary.

179

As the others slowly came to, Adair got up and went to the doors to start unbolting them. Someone outside was persistently knocking, pleading, "Please let me in. If there's anybody here, please let me in."

The old deadbolts were stubborn, not having been unlocked in a long time, but at last Adair got them drawn back and the heavy doors opened. Outside on the front steps was Andi Cain, the girl who had come to see Fletcher yesterday. She looked at Adair rather anxiously as she explained, "He told me to come here."

"Well then, come in!" Adair said, looking around outside. The morning was almost bright gray, but there was a faint red tinge in the sky, in the direction of the Warfield headquarters. There was no one else out on the street. Adair shut the door behind Andi, leaving it unlocked. "Did you talk to Fletcher?" Adair asked her.

"Yeah. I was down at the sheriff's office this morning with my stepmother, Rosie. She's swearing out a restraining order against my dad. I saw Fletcher in the tank there, and he told me to come here. He said I'd be safe here until the train comes," Andi said. As they talked, they moved halfway up the aisle.

"That must mean it's comin' pretty soon," said Cody, coming up to meet them. "Hi, Andi."

"Hi, Cody," she said shyly. "I saw Case there, too, in the tank with Fletcher," she added.

"If the train's coming soon," Adair said to herself, "and Fletcher's still locked up in the sheriff's jail . . . we've got to get him out."

"I don't know about you, but I ain't setting foot out of this place until that train comes," Andi said firmly. "It's gettin' weird out there."

"Weird? How do you mean?" asked Lilith, joining them with a breakfast roll in hand.

"Well, gee, last night I started seeing people that I

hadn't seen in a long time. Remember Grace Hattley, who used to beat her kids with switches all the time?" Andi asked.

"Goodness, I thought that dreadful woman had moved away!" Lilith exclaimed.

"I'd heard that she was living out a ways, but I saw her last night. She came to our door screaming that she couldn't put them down—she had these willow switches *growing* out of her hands! It was so gross. She couldn't get them out of her hands, and she was just covered with welts and scratches. She was all crazy, and Rosie could hardly get her out of the door without getting a lashing herself," Andi related. Adair leaned on a nearby pew for support.

"Several other people came to our door, but Rosie wouldn't open it to anybody after that. I looked out my bedroom window, though, and I saw one of 'em was Jubby Crone," said Andi. Cody took a quick breath.

"Jubby Crone! That's impossible!" Lilith exclaimed.

"I knew nobody'd believe me. But it was Jubby Crone," Andi asserted.

"Who is Jubby Crone?" Adair asked fearfully.

"He died of an overdose a year ago, so he certainly would not be walking around Beaconville last night," Lilith said, affronted.

Cody cleared his throat. "Um, don't bet the farm, Mom. I saw him yesterday, too."

181

11

"Cody Crandall, when did you see Jubby?" Lilith gasped.

"Yesterday, Mom, in the human garbage dump behind that big swank building Fletch showed us. I saw him trying to stick needles in his arms that were 'bout four feet long. He couldn't get a fix and he was just stark raving crazy," Cody said. The others had sat up to listen, except Daniel, who had rolled over and gone back to sleep.

Andi eyed Cody gratefully for backing her up, then looked down when he glanced her way. "Anyhow, if Jubby's on the loose I'm glad to be here," he said.

"My word, this is a nightmare," Lilith breathed. "Do you suppose the—the others we saw there might be out on the streets?"

"Fletch said things would get crazy. I can't remember his exact words, but that's what he meant," Cody said authoritatively, aware of Andi's eyes.

"Then, Cody, get back there and fix that back door! Did you lock the front door?" Lilith demanded of Adair.

She stirred. "Uh, no. No, I didn't." Lilith quickly started toward it but Adair stopped her. "Don't lock it."

"What if all those crazies come here?" Lilith cried.

"I think . . . Fletcher intended for us to let in any- one who wanted to come here—he sent Andi. For some reason we're safe here, and it's not because of the locks. Locking the doors would just keep out the ones who need to be here," Adair argued.

"I wonder," Sophie said from the floor by the vent, "if any of us realizes how close we were to becoming like *them*."

That thought caused a dead silence as they looked around at each other. Lilith abruptly shook her head: "Speak for yourself!"

"I dunno, Mom. You could get real violent when anybody got between you and the TV," Cody offered.

Lilith began angrily, "Cody Crandall, don't you tell me—"

"It doesn't matter now," Adair interrupted, anxious to forestall any ugliness. "All that matters is what we're able to become *now*. Why, Daniel was telling me—" She broke off, looking at the pile of coats where Daniel had been lying. He was gone.

"Daniel," Adair gasped, and the others followed her stare. Sheer terror rose up in her throat to think of him out on the streets with the once-human debris of Beaconville.

"Daniel!" Adair screamed. She ran up the aisle and tore through the doors out onto the front sidewalk.

The change she had barely detected earlier was now startling. The Warfield-fabricated sun had appeared in the sky, poking a hole through the clouds slightly larger than itself—a most unnatural sight. It glowed down on Beaconville with orange-tinted rays, and what little warmth emanated from it was oppressive. The strange heaviness of the air, though no warmer than twenty degrees Fahrenheit, sent Adair staggering back onto the railing of the steps.

Dizzy, she peered down the street and saw a man stumbling up the sidewalk. He too glanced up at the sun, shielding his face, then he darted for shelter into a nearby building. Almost immediately he came out again, cursing in frustration and flailing over his head in a vain attempt to ward off whatever was in the air.

"Adair!" Weaving, she looked back at Lilith standing in the crack of the church door barely open. "Andi found Daniel in the kitchen!"

Nodding, Adair grasped the railing and pulled herself up the steps. It took enormous effort, as if she were swimming against the tide, but she made it to the door and fell in.

It took a few moments for her to recover from the exertion of stepping out. Breathing hard, she looked up at Andi coming into the sanctuary with her arm around Daniel's shoulders. "He was feeding the cat," she said, smiling.

"Nobody fed the kitty yet," he chastened them.

Adair sank into the pew. "That's fine, darling," she panted.

"What's wrong with you?" Lilith asked.

"Andi . . . did you have trouble getting here? Was it hard going?" Adair asked.

"Yeah, now that you mention it. It was like walking in mud the whole way," Andi said.

"Something," Adair gulped, "something really strange is going on out there. Nobody go outside until Fletcher comes."

They eyed her, then looked toward the stained-glass

windows. The windows glowed even under an artificial sun, but showed them nothing of the outside world. The only other window in the small building was in the pastor's study, but it also was stained glass.

"Yeah, okay," Cody said mildly, then turned to Andi. "You want something to eat, or something?"

"Sure," she shrugged, and he took her back to the kitchen to share the stash Fletcher had left for them.

They all ate, then took turns sponge-bathing in the kitchen and the bathroom off the pastor's study. When Adair had Daniel fed and relatively cleaned up (without benefit of fresh clothes, which were still at Lilith's house), she went looking for Sophie. Adair was concerned about her health after the stress of last night.

She found Sophie seated at the desk in the pastor's study, perusing his small library. With a cardigan draped over her shoulders, and her face bathed in the soft glow of the desk lamp, the dear lady looked quite at home among the books. All she needed was Sphinx purring in her lap to complete the picture.

Sophie looked up, taking off a pair of too-large reading glasses, as Adair leaned in the doorway. "I've found some remarkable things here. The last minister kept a journal before he left, and I've been reading it. Here, let me read the last entry to you." Sophie replaced on her nose the glasses the minister had left behind. Holding up a spiral notebook, she began to read: "'Since my awakening, I have labored without success to convince my neighbors that there are actually superior places to live in beyond Beaconville. It sounds absurd to say they don't believe me, because everybody knows someone on the outside; they often get mail and long-distance phone calls from someone out of town. I have observed with particular interest the deliverymen who traffic goods between Beaconville and the outside world:

they have an almost—how can I phrase it—*inhuman* disinterest in anyone or anything but making their deliveries; they will not stay and visit, nor even converse. It is almost as if they are not actually here at all. No one thinks that strange but me.

"'But as the facts remain that no one from the outside ever sets foot here; no one here *now* has ever set foot outside of Beaconville; and no one who left has ever come back, then they have come to believe in their hearts that to leave Beaconville is to die.'"

Adair opened her mouth but Sophie gestured, "There's more: 'Last night, I received a call from Mr. Streiker of Dallas, who told me he is sending a train to Beaconville and wants me on it. When I questioned what would become of the people here if I left, he replied that he himself is coming to see to them, and was quite insistent that I avail myself of this opportunity to escape.

"'So now it comes to this: Do I truly believe there is life on the outside? Do I believe it enough to get on that train? I hear the whistle now; it is sounding as the train pulls up to the station a few blocks away. I have no time to pack clothes or books or anything—

"'I am leaving' . . . and that's all there is," Sophie said quietly. "He did not even take the time to punctuate the last sentence."

With labored breathing, Adair stared at Sophie. "He could hear the train whistle from here," Adair said.

"Yes. The station is a five-minute walk from here. Three if you run," Sophie said. "He used the word *escape*. Your husband knew when he came here the time was short. He knew he would only have a matter of days to convince us to save our own lives."

Adair leaned weakly against the door frame. "I didn't realize any of this," she whispered. "If I had only realized, I would have spent a lot less time arguing with him and done what he asked instead."

Sophie smiled up at her tenderly. The light from her blue eyes surrounded by fragile pink skin made Adair think of the sunshine in Hawaii. "What more could you have done than what you did?" Sophie asked.

As Adair thought this over, they heard voices suddenly raised from the front of the church. With a burst of adrenaline she darted from the study down the short hall into the sanctuary.

She saw Cody and Andi greeting a burly teenager who had just come in. At once she recognized him as the more obnoxious boy at the fast-food restaurant, and she withered slightly. Cody was gleefully inquiring, "Whaddya doin' here, Case, my man?"

Lilith came up to Adair with a pinched face. "I do not want him here!" she hissed.

Adair nodded to her and went forward to listen. "Whoo! Hane out there," Case said, rubbing his red eyes. There was a faint, acrid smell clinging to his rumpled clothes that reminded Adair of the odor from the pits behind the Warfield complex.

"What are you doing here?" Lilith asked in an accusatory voice from behind Adair.

"Well, see, I was at the sheriff's office to see a home-slice," Case began.

"Slice of what?" interrupted Lilith.

"A friend, Mom. Chill, please," Cody whispered.

"Case McCrea, you are such a liar. You were in jail for robbing the drugstore," Lilith retorted, still safely behind Adair.

Case's freckled face reddened slightly in anger, then he jerked his head indifferently. "Okay, so I was in the tank. What of it? Last night they brought in this straight dude who told me to come here."

"Fletcher?" Adair said eagerly. "You talked to Fletcher?"

"Yeah, we shot the gift for some long time," Case said, his hard face relaxing. "He's . . . not like I was looking for in a suit. He was—phat, man, like nobody else I seen. Anyway, this a.m. he sprang me and told me to appear here."

"How'd he get you out?" Cody asked.

Case paused. "You'll think I'm shady."

"Try me!" Cody dared him, and the others listened intently.

"See, here are the sheriff an' the mayor blizzing to find the right type of gas mask for whatever's pollutin' the air and they just left us easin' in the tank there. The stink's in all the buildings too, except this one. Random, dude. So, when everybody had gone, the man gets up and says, 'Let's go.'

"And I'm like, 'You got a key on you, guy?' and so he. . . ." Case faltered, looking at their expectant faces. "So he walked right through them bars like they was nothing. They just crumbled right around him and you can put that on the set," he affirmed solemnly. *Just like the Warfield building!* Adair thought.

"Think it ain't," Cody agreed, nodding.

Looking surprised and heartened that no one sneered at him, Case continued, "So, then he tells me to come to the church. He had to jet to a JO—"

"What?" Adair interrupted sharply.

"He had other things to take care of," Cody told her.

Case continued, "Yeah, but he says I'd find home-skillets here ["Friends," Cody translated quietly], and he says that we was to run get on the train when we hear the whistle, even if it's, like, really deep in the p.m."

"That's what he told me, too," Andi said.

Case turned to her. "He shoot the gift with you?"

189

While they shared stories of what Fletcher had told them, Lilith pulled Adair aside. She checked to see Daniel close by, watching Case from behind a pew, then listened to Lilith protest, "I don't want him here with us. He's a hoodlum."

"I can't turn him out when Fletcher sent him," Adair murmured. "But I can make some things clear to him—if he understands English."

She went over to the teenagers, interrupting, "Case." He turned to her. "Since Fletcher sent you, you're welcome here. But you have to respect the others who are here. Fletcher wouldn't sit still for a repeat performance of what we saw at the restaurant."

He flushed. "You're juiced with me, Mom duke," he muttered.

Adair glanced at Cody, who subtly nodded to confirm that Case intended to cooperate. "He must've whipped your *okole*," Adair observed, flexing a jargon that *he* wouldn't know. The shift in his present attitude from the defiant punk at the restaurant was near miraculous.

Case grinned fleetingly, catching the gist. "Yeah, he . . . he showed me some dudes I used to know. Some guys I used to think coldblooded. Really cool, you know." He began making an effort to talk without the obscure jargon. "We used to say we was gonna live fast, die young, and leave a beautiful corpse. So the man showed me their corpses, and they was not beautiful. The heinous thing was, they was calling for me to join them. 'Hey, Case!' they said. 'Let's scam.' And these are like, rottin' cretin maggots by now. [Cody nodded in sudden recollection.] So the man says to me, 'You gonna stay with them, Case, or you gonna come with me?' And I says, 'I'm Audi five thousand dudes.' That's when he tells me to hike it here."

"Okay," she nodded and smiled. "Good."

Turning away, Adair saw that Sophie had come into the auditorium to listen. Adair said to her, "Before all this, I was coming to see how you felt. How are your legs this morning?"

"Better, better," Sophie assured her. She took a few slow steps, but without a limp. "I hope I won't be a burden getting to the train," she added apprehensively.

"I'll help you, Sophie," Daniel piped up, crawling up on the back of a pew to put his arms around Adair's neck.

"Thank you, dear," Sophie said, her eyes glistening. Looking at her eyes, Adair then thought of the rain in Hawaii. Sophie saw her pensive expression and queried, "Yes?"

Adair shook her head. "Every time I look at you, I think about Hawaii."

Sophie put a hand to the crinkly skin at her throat. "I remind you of Hawaii? How interesting. You know, I feel in some strange way that . . . I'm already there," she whispered.

The idea surprised Adair, then she mused, "Why not? It's clear your heart's not here anymore."

With moist, expectant eyes, Sophie looked up to windows she could not see through and said, "I can't wait to see it in person."

At that point Daniel saw Sphinx creeping out from under a pew where she had been hiding. As Daniel clambered down to lovingly pursue her, Adair said, "Go anywhere in the church, Daniel, but *don't go outside*."

He looked back in utter obedience, promising, "I won't, Mom duke." Adair smiled and winced.

Over the next few hours they found diverse means of occupying themselves. Daniel and Sphinx discovered many interesting objects to play with in the kitchen; Cody, Case, and Andi sequestered themselves in teen talk; Lilith and Sophie returned to investigate the study; and Adair kept watch over them all. While Fletcher was absent, she felt responsible for them.

Somewhere around noon the teens were first to raid the refrigerator. Case, however, self-consciously rejected everything but a roll and water.

The others soon began to drift in looking for something to eat. "Without my soap operas, I didn't know when it was time for lunch," Lilith joked lamely. "It could be four o'clock, for all I know."

"Yeah, you wonder," Cody said, looking restlessly toward the door. "I'm getting a little crazy to see what's happening outside."

"Don't go out, Cody," Adair urgently warned.

"I won't, I won't. But—what harm would it do to just open the door and look? Is that gonna kill us, to look out?" he asked.

Adair hesitated just long enough for him to decide to do it. As they had firmly secured the back door, he went to the large double doors at the rear of the sanctuary. Anxiously, Adair and Andi followed him. Case looked on with low-grade interest.

Cody grasped the handle and pushed on the door enough to open it six inches, peering out. "Wow," he breathed, and the others crowded close to see out around him.

It was snowing now. But the virgin white snow from last night was gone; mixed with the pollution from the Warfield pits, the descending snow was an unnerving light red, like bloody water. Snowdrifts on the ground were the splotchy red of diseased skin. That acrid smell pervaded the air, and the sun was a dim ball behind weird purple clouds, bruises across the sky.

They stared in the fascination of horror. Then Andi

gasped, "Someone's coming! Shut the door!" The impulse was understandable, given the appearance of the man lunging down the sidewalk toward the church. He was obviously in dire straits, hardly able to wheeze for the cold and the toxic air. His mottled skin hung on a gaunt frame, and his eyes rolled wildly as he clutched his coat, searching for shelter.

All that would have been troublesome enough, but he had another problem. He was lunging because of the load he was dragging behind him. They could not see what it was, but it was clearly an unwelcome burden—he kept kicking at it to try to dislodge it. As he was not touching it with his hands, it was unclear how it was connected to him.

They watched breathlessly while he came closer and closer. Andi finally hid her face in Adair's back, Cody seemed unable to shut the door, and no one else moved.

At last he came to the steps of the church. But he did not slow down or even look aside—it was as if he did not see them at all. As he lumbered painfully past, Cody uttered, "Good gosh! That's—"

Before he said more Adair saw what he was lugging behind him. It was the body of a man, fully clothed, limp as sand, with a bright red stain covering its entire front. It stubbornly scooted down the icy sidewalk as if magnetically attached to its host, changing positions as it was kicked.

When the unfortunate resident had passed on with his burden, Cody came to himself and quickly shut the door. "Thank God he didn't see us," he gasped.

"Was that—?" Case began, so pale that his freckles stood out.

"That was Bedletter. As bad as he looked, I'd know him anywhere," Cody vowed.

"Who's Bedletter?" Adair asked.

"Meanest dude I ever met in my life. He was convicted of murdering Cliff Sanders during a dogfight. Stabbed him in the chest eleven times. He was s'posed t'have been shipped off to state prison," Cody said, shaking.

"The body," Adair murmured numbly. "Did you recognize the body behind him . . . ?"

"I couldn't be sure—but—that couldn't be. Cliff was killed at least three years ago," Cody gulped.

They stared at each other with only the sound of breathing in their ears as Adair reached another plateau of understanding. It was bad enough being trapped in a place of such relentless decay, but what was more unsettling was the permanence of it. Here, the consequences of every rash act hung over one like a neon advertisement. Even such inner states as laziness, greed, or duplicity were broadcast without consent. There was no such thing as a private thought when what you were on the inside was so blatantly displayed on the outside. This was what Adair found most terrifying about the town.

Then Andi, childlike, reassured herself, "He didn't see us."

"No, he never saw us," Adair echoed. "And I bet . . . he hasn't talked to Fletcher yet, either. Fletcher would never let him in here carrying that thing behind him."

"Look, I don't see any reason to tell my mom about this, okay? It would only scare her," Cody said seriously.

"No problemo, guy," Case said, gripping his shoulder.

"No need," Adair agreed, turning to look for Daniel. At once she thought about her father on the streets somewhere, and her heart broke.

For a long time after that, they all took refuge in their individual interests, expressing no desire to see what was happening outside. After a few minutes a bored Andi drifted into the study where Sophie sat at the minister's desk. "Whatcha reading?" Andi asked.

Sophie lifted her face. "A book of sermons," she replied.

"Oh." Andi winced, backing away.

"It's just a little book—barely a hundred and fifty pages," Sophie said, laying it thoughtfully aside. "But it has made some things clear to me that I never understood before."

"What?" Andi asked in mild curiosity.

"Oh, that we were never meant to be here. We were never meant to—to digress to this point. But since we did, it required a massive intervention to set us right," Sophie said. "Can you imagine what it would be like to be happy—to never be afraid—to have what you always wanted even when you're not sure what that is?"

"No," Andi said flatly.

"But he talks as if that's a certainty," Sophie said, lifting the book. "Listen to this: 'On a beautiful morning in August I saw three shepherds come from the Syrian hills with their little flocks. They met in the narrow valley, and the herds mingled while the shepherds exchanged their morning greetings. In a few moments one of the herdsmen left the other two, and as he went he gave a meaningless yodel, but what magic power that call had on his little flock! The last one of his sheep left the mingled herd and followed the shepherd; and he did not stop to count them, so sure was he that they knew him and would follow him. . . . The call rings out above the roar of the storm to quiet the distressed and troubled children. Their names have not only been written on His ledger, they have been engraved on the palms of His hands. And the decree has gone out, "That where I am, there you may be also."'"

"You mean, he's not talking about sheep, but people," Andi said.

"Yes. And he implies there are joys we can't even imagine," said Sophie.

"I can't imagine what," Andi said.

"That's right!" Sophie laughed. Drawn by the sound, Adair leaned in the doorway to listen. Sophie went on, "We've gotten so used to the pitiful conditions here that we think the whole universe must be the same. Why can't we imagine anything good? Why can't we visualize life outside Beaconville?"

"Maybe because you've never had anything to compare it with," Adair offered.

"And yet, the library has scads of travelogues," Sophie countered.

"Everybody I know thinks they're just made up," Andi said.

"That's because you can't convince somebody with words what they have to experience to believe," Adair said. "I could talk all day about Manoa Valley, Tantalus Drive, and Hanauma Bay—even show you pictures—but it doesn't mean anything to you until you've been there." Seeing the pictures of Hawaii in Fletcher's file folder had convinced her of that. Theoretically, Adair knew that such a place existed, but the heady sensation of *being* there, of *living* there, was incomprehensible to her until Fletcher brought her there himself.

"Well, *anything's* better than Beaconville," Andi declared, slumping down in the one chair opposite the pastor's desk.

"And isn't it gracious of Fletcher to take us with him when we can't come up with any better reason to go," Sophie said quietly.

"Adair!" Lilith's panicky voice screeched from down the hall. She momentarily pounced on Adair, squeezing her arm fearfully. "Somebody just came in wearing a gas mask, and I don't think Fletcher sent him!"

Adair gave her a pat of reassurance and strode down to the sanctuary. Entering, she saw the man who had just come in pause to remove his ineffectual gas mask. It was Gus Gramble. Again.

He turned red, watering eyes on Adair and said, "Your husband busted out of jail this morning. I've been deputized to bring him back in, and I just thought he might be here."

⚜ 12 ⚜

A dair returned Gus's level gaze and said, "Fletcher is not here."

"Well—" Gus was interrupted by a mild coughing fit, then painfully cleared his throat and resumed, "maybe you've seen Case McCrea. He seems to have disappeared at about the same time." Ironically, both Cody and Case seemed to have disappeared at Gus's entrance, while Andi and Sophie had followed Adair from the study to stand behind her.

There was no question about Adair's telling the truth. "Case is here. Fletcher sent him here, so you're not taking him anywhere," she said.

"McCrea was in official custody, and I got to take him back. If you interfere, I'm authorized to take you in as well," Gus threatened, wheezing. Lilith began whimpering. Fortunately, Daniel was in the kitchen and did not hear this interchange.

"I don't think so," Adair said drily. There was a

certain suspicion in the back of her mind that he could probably take her out by force, but she determined to make it as difficult for him as possible.

"I'm sorry to hear you say that; I really am," Gus said, drawing a deep breath. Then he seemed to notice that he had breathed without pain. Glancing around the sanctuary, he said, "It's clean in here."

"That's right. That's one reason Fletcher sent us here. You . . . can stay if you want," Adair said cautiously, and Lilith threw up her hands in dismay.

Gus looked at her ironically. "You just goin' to stay here until it clears up outside?"

"No. We're going to stay here until the train comes. We're leaving on the Morning Sun. Fletcher has bought tickets for anyone in Beaconville to leave on it," Adair told him.

"Why don't you just tell him to help himself from the fridge?" Lilith hissed in her ear.

"We'll see about that." Gus smiled tightly. "Now, if you don't mind, I'm going to have a look back there." He moved toward the aisle, and Adair stepped out to block him.

With a derisive snort he grabbed her elbow, and Adair tensed for a fight. Then the door behind him opened, and a guy with a handkerchief covering his face leaned in. "Gus, they found the Streiker fella at the movie house talking to a bunch of folks, big as you please."

Gus glanced over his shoulder, reluctantly releasing Adair's arm. He promised her in a low voice, "If Case ain't with him, I'll be back." Then he unconsciously took a sustaining breath before shouldering his way out the door.

Those inside were silent for a time, until Sophie asked, "How could you find it in yourself to stand up to him like that, Adair? And for Case, of all people?"

She was surprised at first, then shrugged. "I don't know. Gus doesn't scare me. He's . . . he's not the enemy. He's just somebody else who's drowning and doesn't know it."

"If he's not the 'enemy,' then who is?" Lilith asked, almost offended by such absurdity.

Adair paused, groping for words. "It's—it's an influence we can't really see and touch. I think that if we could, just the sight of it would kill us."

"I was not allowed to see everything at the pits," Sophie added. "That must be why. If there are some things too wonderful for us to imagine, then it follows that there are also things too horrible for us to imagine."

Adair was concurring when Cody peeked around the corner. "He gone?" he whispered.

"Yeah, you can tell the Mighty Chipmunk to come out of hiding. Adair scared him off," Andi replied sarcastically.

Cody looked abashed, but a minute later Case sauntered in. "And who came calling?" he asked casually.

"What a wimp!" Andi snorted.

"Gus Gramble, saying he's going to lock both of us up," Adair said ruefully, then added, "I, for one, don't see what he can do. So Fletcher's out talking to people, huh?" It tickled her—the idea of Fletcher roaming free, doing what he came to do while Gus and his buddies flailed around trying to stop him. Smiling to herself, she went to check on Daniel.

Less than an hour later they began to get an inkling of what Gus could do. Adair was in the sanctuary with Daniel, looking through a hymnal left on the floor, when shadows passing over the stained glass windows caught her eye. She paused, then called, "Sophie! Lilith!"

Those two came in, followed by the others who had heard Adair calling. Nodding toward a window, she said, "A number of people are going back and forth around the building."

They watched for a minute more, then Cody exclaimed, "I smell kerosene!"

"They're going to burn us out!" cried Lilith.

Daniel flung his arms around Adair's neck and she clutched him. There was a momentary silence outside, then a whoosh, and the silhouette of dancing flames appeared on the windows.

"We gotta bus one!" Case shouted.

"Leave?" demanded Adair. "Where would we go?"

"I dunno, Mom duke, but it's L-twelve to sit here!" Case yelled, streaking down the aisle. He flung himself out the doors into the red street.

Cody began after him. "Cody! Wait!" Adair barked. He looked back at her wildly and she demanded, "Wouldn't Fletcher know about this? Wouldn't he tell us what we needed to do?"

It was enough to make him pause. Meanwhile, Adair stubbornly resisted the intense urge to panic and run as Case had done. She sat right there in the pew holding Daniel. When common sense had dictated flight in similar circumstances once before, Adair had lost no time getting herself and Daniel out. But now they were in a realm where the events that took place before their very eyes contradicted common sense and previous experience. In such circumstances all she had to rely on was what Fletcher said. He had said to wait here, so wait she would.

Her intransigence restrained the others from rushing out. They waited in fearful stillness, watching for smoke or flames to begin slithering through cracks or around corners.

There was some commotion outside—no one could tell if it had to do with Case or not—but minutes passed and the silhouetted flames began subsiding. There had been no breach in the stone walls of the church. But Case did not come back.

Those inside stirred cautiously, looking at each other. "I don't smell kerosene anymore. I don't smell anything," Cody said.

"They couldn't get it to burn," Sophie said with a quiver of triumph.

But there was hardly any opportunity to celebrate. Someone suddenly rattled the front doors, then pounded on them. "Open up! Sheriff's department!" a loud voice demanded.

Dumbstruck, the group looked at the doors. Not only had no one locked them, but they could see from where they stood that the doors were unbolted.

"Open up *now*!" the voice shouted.

"They're unlocked!" Adair called.

The doors were then fiercely beaten and rattled. Being outward-opening doors, it was useless to try to batter them in, but someone came up with another tack. A burst of automatic gunfire pelted the door and the locks.

Everybody inside the sanctuary hit the carpet. When the gunfire was unsuccessful in splintering the door, it was directed against several of the stained-glass windows. Daniel covered his ears from the piercing *ratatatatat* that hammered the leaded windows.

There was a sudden quiet. Breathless, everyone looked up from the floor. Not one window had been broken by the assault. Jesus still stood at the door and carried the sheep on His shoulders.

One by one, they all got up and looked around. "They can't get in," Sophie said. "They can't force us out." This much was undeniable.

"How was Gus able to walk in earlier if they can't get in now?" Lilith asked, perplexed. Adair shook her head without answering. She had an idea, but was too distracted to put it in words.

"Daddy won't let them in unless they'll be nice," Daniel said, stiff-lipped. Nobody scoffed.

They sat there for a long time, waiting, while darkness surrounded the church outside and the motel's neon lights came on. After not hearing anything for over an hour, Adair finally got up and went to the doors, putting a hand on the handle. "Don't!" Lilith urged in a horrified hiss. Adair hesitated, then turned the handle and opened the door.

The darkness outside was like nothing she had ever seen. It was a palpable darkness, a lead curtain that extended in all directions from the threshold of the church. Adair could not see the street or anything across it. Although she could see the motel lights through the window, she could not see them from the doorstep. She could not see the snow or how red the air was. Looking down, she could not see anything beyond her feet.

She stretched her arm out in front of her and felt nothing. She could see her hand but nothing around it, as if it rested on a featureless black canvas.

The silence was as dense as the darkness. Adair heard nothing—no motors, no animal sounds, not even the wind. Quietly, she withdrew back into the auditorium and shut the door. "I don't see much need for a walk tonight," she said drily.

"What happened to Case?" Cody asked in a child's voice.

"I imagine they put him back in jail," Adair said.

Cody sat, biting his lip. Lilith wavered, then came

over and sat down beside him, opening her arms. Cody put his head on her shoulder and cried. Daniel knuckled his eyes in sympathy and reached up to Adair's neck.

"What happens if the train comes tonight? What if we have to get there through *that*?" Andi asked, jerking her head toward the blackness beyond the doors.

"I . . . don't know," Adair said. "All I know is that Fletcher went to a lot of trouble to get us this far. He's not going to strand us here now." This seemed a reasonable assumption, even to Lilith.

So those six and Sphinx shared a subdued, grateful dinner of cold sandwiches, crackers, and hot cocoa in the kitchen, then they settled down beside the sanctuary floor vents in groups: Adair, Daniel, and Sophie sat around one, while Lilith, Cody, and Andi gathered around the one across the room. Even with Adair and his friends bunny and blankie protecting him, Daniel was too frightened to let anyone dim the sanctuary lights to sleep. So they were obliged to wait for him to nod off first.

From the floor beside Daniel, Adair looked up to the now-familiar window of Jesus at the door. After a moment she squinted and frowned, studying it more closely. It looked different from before. The face of Jesus looked different— it had more expression, more vitality. There was an urgency in the features that had not been present before; and, strangely, His hair was shorter and darker. There was a vague familiarity about Him. . . . Adair's eyes traveled to His hand resting on the doorknob and she gasped. The door was open a crack. He was no longer knocking, but in the process of gently opening the door. She was sure the picture had not been that way at first.

Turning, she stared at the companion window

across the room, that of Jesus carrying the lamb on His shoulders. Not being as familiar with this window, she couldn't positively say that it had changed, but she felt that it had. There was that remarkably lifelike expression on His face, in this case a knowing halfsmile—now *who* did that remind her of? And in addition to the lamb on His shoulders, there were other sheep following Him that she had not noticed at first.

She studied the lamb that rested across His shoulders. In typical shepherd fashion, He held it in place with one hand gripping its forelegs and the other its hind legs. It was certainly a confining position for the lamb, who couldn't move anything but its head. But it kept the lamb from panicking, kicking out of the Shepherd's grasp and falling off His shoulders. Having no choice but to be still, the lamb lay contentedly in what the other sheep might very well view as a cushy position. Gazing at the window, Adair thought, *Does that lamb realize how much He loves her?*

Seeing that Daniel was finally asleep, Cody got up and dimmed the sanctuary lights to a soft yellow glow. The windows covered themselves in darkness for the night, and Adair lay down thinking about the lamb.

✳

"Adair. Adair." She opened bleary eyes at Sophie and Lilith bending over her.

Mumbling an acknowledgment, Adair hoisted herself up on an elbow and blinked around at the brightness of the auditorium. "The sun must be out this morning," she noted drowsily. Daniel was still asleep, with his blankie spread over his face.

"That's what we want you to look at. Something's

happening outside and we want to know what it is," Lilith said in an edgy whisper. Without benefit of curlers, her brown hair lay flat against her head. From force of habit she self-consciously fluffed it once or twice.

"You haven't looked outside yourself?" Adair asked, sitting up and stretching her creaky back.

"No. All we've seen is that," Sophie said, pointing. Adair squinted at the windows.

It was definitely brighter outside, as the colors in the glass panes glowed. But every now and then fist-sized shadows passed across the windows from top to bottom. "What on earth is that?" Adair asked.

"That's what we want you to find out. Now go look," Lilith urged.

Adair got to her feet and went down the aisle toward the doors. Daniel did not stir; nor did Cody and Andi, still curled up beside the opposite grate. Adair reached the door, turned the handle, and opened it up to look out.

It was still very cold outside. The Warfield sun, glowing a yellow-orange, had cleared the sky of clouds. But in the distance, directly under the sun, an ominous red ocean was visible on the horizon. It was the mass from the pits.

As Adair looked, a red ball sailed down from the sky and splattered on the steps at her feet. It was a stinking, viscous, boiling liquid. Adair jumped back to prevent it from getting on her boots. As she watched, a half dozen similar projectiles hit the street and sidewalk. One landed on the roof of the building across the street, and in a moment Adair saw flames shoot up from the spot. Stepping as far out on the street as she dared, she saw smoke rising from several points beyond the church. Edwina Moos and her art gallery sprang to mind, and Adair ironically wondered how she would adjust the thermostat to compensate for her gallery burning down.

She quickly closed the door. "It's from the pits. The pits are overflowing this way," she announced calmly.

"When is that train coming?" Lilith asked in a low voice that rose with panic. "What if it's already left without us?"

"He won't leave us here!" Adair insisted, glancing at the window of the shepherd for support.

"How will we get there with that stuff flying around? It will fry us!" Lilith cried, and the children began to stir.

Adair just looked at her. "I can't believe you're throwing such a fit over a little red mud when fire and bullets couldn't touch us. Now, have you fed Sphinx this morning?"

Lilith's eyelids fluttered wildly for a moment, then she said, "No, I haven't," and turned up the aisle toward the kitchen, Sphinx meowing at her heels.

Daniel suddenly sat up and removed the baby blanket from his face to run after Lilith into the kitchen. "I wanna feed the kitty! Let me feed the kitty!" That sufficiently roused Andi and Cody, who also thought of breakfast right away.

Sophie paused, then murmured discreetly, "I think I will use the minister's facilities before a crowd forms at the door." She went out, leaving Adair alone in the sanctuary.

Adair dropped into a pew, touching her greasy hair. A bath might help her feel a little cleaner in this grungy town. She looked up at the window with the tender-eyed shepherd. Studying it, she whispered, "What are *you* doing here? How did *you* ever come to such a place?"

Almost as if hearing a reply, she looked at the third

window, to the left of the dais at the front of the auditorium. This was the universally recognizable picture of Jesus on the cross.

Adair got up to stand in front of that window, unconsciously folding her arms. There was the head, bleeding under the ring of thorns, bowed in pain. There were the spikes through the wrists that caused the fingers to claw. There was the lean body twisted unnaturally to fit the instrument of torture. *Nothing unusual here*, Adair thought.

But as she continued to gaze, she became aware of an undercurrent—so slight that at first she thought it was only the beating of her heart. When it gained force and resonance she put her hand on the window, wondering if it were pulsing. It felt warm to the touch.

Adair stepped back, peering at the window. Her eyes went to the bowed head. Although His face was obscured by the angle, she saw something in it besides pain: intense concentration. Force of will. Clearly, He was doing something other than just hang there. Adair's eyes were drawn to the sky above His head. In the middle of the sky was the curious depiction of a break that she had first assumed to be lead. But it wasn't; it was drawn into the glass. That break, emanating from above the central figure, ran down from the sky to split the ground beyond the cross. It was like . . . a cataclysmic disruption in the natural world. A mighty break in the currents.

There was a tiny little detail in the window that Adair almost missed. Glimpsing an apparently misplaced piece of red, she leaned close to the window to trace the leading with her finger. There—at the edge of the window, a spot of red could be seen atop the break. What did it mean? Was it something coming out of the break, something being sucked into it, or something beyond it? Adair shook her head and stepped back to take in the window as a whole. And what she saw now was an unequivocal display of power.

"Mommy, ain't you gonna come have some breakas?" Daniel asked from behind her.

Adair turned to see him enter the sanctuary, his little face smeared with powerful amounts of sweet-roll glazing. "Sure," she murmured. "If you saved me any, that is."

"You can share mine." He offered up the sticky remains of sweet roll.

Adair took a bite, laughing, "Thanks," and Daniel, pleased, escorted her to the kitchen.

Following breakfast, Adair began her second straight day in the church by washing her hair in the minister's lavatory with hand soap. That helped her feel so much better that she endeavored to convince Daniel of the comforts of cleanliness, but he ran to hide under a pew.

The others were beginning to get restless as well. "How long d'you suppose we gotta wait here?" Cody complained.

"Till Fletcher comes, whenever that is," Adair said.

"What if the whistle blows and he hasn't come yet?" Cody asked.

Adair thought it over. "Then we go to the train. He was pretty firm on that."

"And what if that stuff starts coming down harder?" Lilith asked fearfully.

"Look." Adair put her hands up in resignation. "I can't guess what's going to happen. I can't predict what Fletcher will do. But when the time comes to go, we'll know it and we'll be able to get there. That's all I'm going to say about that."

"So there!" Daniel added for emphasis from underneath a pew.

Adair reached down and seized a little foot. "Gotcha! You get to come with me, now!" Daniel kicked and howled, but a mother intent on imposing cleanliness is not easily dissuaded. Daniel got his bath in the sink.

After everyone had eaten and more or less washed up, they drifted back to the sanctuary, as it was the most comfortable place in the building to wait. Cody seemed especially in need of comfort this morning. He slumped at a pew by himself sullenly drumming a hymnal in his lap. His hair lay in heavy clumps and his clothes had taken on a powerful air.

Lilith's face registered her dismay as she regarded him. Watching, Adair could almost see her thinking, *Why do you have to dress like that? Why won't you clean yourself up? Why can't you sit up straight and smile now and then?*

But then Lilith did an amazing thing. Absently fluffing her flat, stringy hair, she went over and sat down beside her son. He glanced up and she smiled at him. Then she said, "I was so proud of you the other night for getting us here. I don't think any of us would've made it here without you." He looked up with slightly widened eyes and she insisted, "I'm real proud of you, Cody."

In response, Cody offered her a genuine smile without smirking, and then laid his head on her shoulder without shame. Lilith put her arms around him, looking up to one of the windows with moist eyes. The bracelet on her arm that Fletcher had bought her reflected golden glints from the window. It made Adair recall something Fletcher had said about someone who ached to have Lilith's arms around him.

"I'm scared for Case," Cody quietly admitted.

"I know," Lilith murmured.

211

Adair raised her eyes to the window, watching the shadows of red hail fall with greater force and frequency. There was no telling now what would become of Case—or Daynell or Jerry or any of the others who had refused Fletcher's offer of shelter. She looked around at Andi and Sophie sitting together reading books they'd found in the minister's study, and at Daniel tempting Sphinx with a loose string from his sweater. It was disheartening to think that out of all the residents of Beaconville, Fletcher had managed to lure only four to the safety of the church. She wouldn't presume to call the percentage a failure, but four out of several thousand seemed hardly worthwhile. Unless, of course, you were one of the four.

After a while, Sophie finished the book and laid it on the pew. Rubbing her eyes, she looked down at the hymnal beside her and picked that up. She thumbed through it, pausing occasionally to hum a familiar tune. (There was a piano tucked off to the side of the dais, but no one here knew how to play it.) She stopped on one particular page, staring down at the words for a long time. Then she began to sing them to herself.

She sang softly, so as not to disturb anyone else. But one by one the others stopped what they were doing to listen to her. Although she sang in a wavering voice, not entirely on key, by the last stanza, everyone else was hanging on each graceful word:

"When ends life's transient dream,
When death's cold, sullen stream
Shall o'er me roll,
Blest Saviour, then, in love,
Fear and distrust remove;
O bear me safe above,
A ransomed soul!"

For a few silent moments following, the sanctuary was brighter and lighter than it had been. Then they all returned to their separate concerns.

They waited in the makeshift train station. Thinking about that, Adair voiced, "I wonder why Fletcher didn't have us just wait *at* the train station."

Sophie raised her head. "It's small and dirty and never open when it's supposed to be. I'd certainly rather wait here. It's close enough."

"It would be nice if he'd just drop by to check on us," Andi said, taking up the thought from Adair's brain. "Wonder what's keeping him. Do you suppose he's bringing the train?"

Adair shrugged. "I don't know. I got the impression it was coming at a certain time that he had nothing to do with."

"Oh," said Andi. "Weird. I wish it would go ahead and come."

"Yeah, I'm tired of waiting," Cody muttered.

"The groceries are getting low," Lilith noted.

"Crudbuckets, what if this goes on for another week?" Cody moaned.

Adair looked toward the windows again. "It can't," she argued. "The overflow from the pits is coming too quickly. It—" She broke off in shock.

Lilith looked where Adair was staring at the window and asked, "What is it?"

Blanching, Adair got up and knelt close in front of Jesus with the sheep. Around the edges of the window, a tiny bit of thick red gunk was oozing in.

❧ 13 ❧

While Adair gazed at the window, trying to comprehend it, Sophie came over and looked. "So it's getting in here, too," she commented flatly. "I suppose it was just a matter of time."

Lilith rushed over to look, almost knocking Sophie aside. About a tablespoon of the thick red stuff bubbled through a tiny crack between the leading and casing of the window. "It's coming in! We're going to get eaten up!" she cried.

Cody reached out to her. "Mom—"

"We're going to die in those pits!" Lilith cried, on the verge of hysteria.

"We're not, Mom! Fletch is coming and we're leaving on the train!" Cody insisted, grabbing her arms.

"Where is he? What if he doesn't get here in time?" Lilith asked. She was shaking all over.

The ground reeling under her, Adair turned from

the window and saw Daniel. She fixed her eyes on him to remind herself how much Fletcher loved him—how much he had risked to make sure Daniel would be with him. After all that, she had to believe Fletcher would not let anything here touch him. Hadn't Fletcher already said he was not in danger?

Daniel himself did not look frightened. At this moment he was preoccupied with the window on the right of the dais—the one depicting Jesus on the white horse. Daniel was studying it as if it had just walked in and presented itself as something new. Adair followed his gaze to the window.

This she had to assume was Jesus. Although the facial features were slightly different from those in any of the other windows, the purposeful expression was consistent. He wore an armor breastplate over a white tunic with red edges, and on His leggings was lettering indecipherable to Adair. The horse He sat on was rearing to accommodate the vertical space of the window. Beyond that, there appeared to be nothing remarkable about it.

In the bottom corners of the window were two letters she believed she recognized: A and Ω—alpha and omega, the first and the last, the beginning and the end. She looked up at the face again, and there was that indefinable something, a familiarity that whispered her name.

"Who are You?" she whispered in return.

"Talking to picture windows, Adair?" Cody taunted weakly.

She did not hear him, concentrating as she was on a concept larger than anything she had ever tried to grasp before. It contained an area greater than Beaconville, Dallas, and Hawaii. It encompassed events from long before she was born till long after she would die . . . from the beginning to the end.

Her eyes went hollow. "None of this is really happening," she said flatly. "I am dreaming."

"Thanks a lot," Cody said sarcastically. "Then would you mind checking me out of your dream?"

"Then it doesn't matter what we do. As far as you're concerned, it doesn't matter what happens to us," Lilith said bitterly to her. Sophie studied Adair as if concerned for her state of mind.

"No," Adair said, turning. "Somehow, the choices we make now are . . . critical. But everything else is just—smoke and mirrors. It's not real."

The others looked at each other cautiously. Sophie said carefully, "We don't know what you mean."

Adair suddenly went over to the leaking window and wiped up the red goo with her fingers. Lilith gasped. Turning, Adair showed them her hand. The goo had disappeared, leaving no marks behind. "Remember the Warfield building?" she said.

They stared in confounded silence. "This is way bizarre," Cody finally observed.

"Fletcher assured me Daniel is not in danger. And if he's not in danger, then neither are we. The reason is, what we're seeing and experiencing is not real. Daniel even said you all were not real," Adair said.

"Thanks, guy," Cody said sarcastically to Daniel, who looked unperturbed.

Adair shook her head. "I don't mean that you don't exist. I mean that . . . that somehow this has all been set up as a—a picture, an illustration of how important our choices are. When I wake up, and when you wake up, we'll all be back in our regular lives, faced with the regular decisions we have to make every day. Somebody wanted to show us that those little decisions mean a lot more than we ever realized."

They all still looked at her blankly. Adair inhaled. "Think about it! What was Fletcher asking? He asked Jerry to stop doing business with unscrupulous suppliers; he asked Daynell to get rid of dishonesty in her store; he asked Lilith to forgive her ex-husband; and he asked me . . . to watch and learn," she said on a lower note. "But he admitted his main goal was to *get us out of here*—to make us willing to leave a state that would destroy us in the end. But he's not talking about Beaconville as a place—he's talking about what's *inside* of us! He wants to get Beaconville out from *inside* us!"

They still looked at her. Andi said, "Then what does it matter if we get on the train or not?"

"It matters more than anything else we'll ever do. It's just that—the obstacles that would prevent us— that make everyone else here so sick—are no more real than that big, fancy Warfield building," Adair said.

"When we were there, he said that if we went there without him it would shut up on us like a steel trap," Sophie recalled.

Adair nodded, returning to the window of the conqueror. "When you're in the middle of a nightmare, it's as real as anything to you. But when the sun rises, and you wake up, you realize you were trapped in nothing more than shadows. But . . . you have to be willing to wake up and face the light. You'll never get free of the nightmares if you won't wake up."

She reached out and touched the window, tracing the red along the lower edge of the tunic He wore. The red was carefully painted in irregular lines to demonstrate that it was not a decorative border on the tunic— it was a stain from the field of battle, a definite sign that He had seen the worst of the conflict, had walked where it was bloodiest. "You have been here," she said in a low voice.

"You're weird," Cody observed. "But I'm gonna be the first on that train," he confirmed.

"Right behind me," Andi said archly.

From that point on, they began waiting with real expectancy. Nobody particularly fretted when they ran out of fruit, and nobody showed extreme alarm when the red slime began oozing through a crack in another window. Sophie, finding the sight objectionable, did take the trouble to mop it up with paper towels (*not* her fingers). So Cody found some putty under the sink in the kitchen and sealed over both cracks in twenty seconds.

Lilith sat on a pew stroking Sphinx, who purred like a steam engine in her lap. With guilty regret, she said, "I suppose I shouldn't bother bringing her on the train. She's just a dumb animal and doesn't know anything about dishonesty or forgiveness."

"Maybe not, but she'd learn a lot about cruelty and neglect if you left her. She's dependent on you. Fletcher must have intended for you to bring her, because he bought the cat food and kitty litter," Adair reminded her.

"That's right," Lilith said, brightening. She snuggled the cat to her face, and Sphinx opened one eye in displeasure.

They waited patiently enough through the hours, watching without alarm as the shadows of hail descended across the windows outside with greater frequency. Adair slipped into a reverie thinking about the times she had waited for Fletcher before: waiting in her tiny Wilderness Trails apartment for him to make good on his proposal; waiting at the Whinnets' house for him to come meet Daniel. Waiting was easier now that she knew him better. There was absolutely no doubt in her mind that he was good as his word.

Watching Daniel roll on the floor underneath the

pews, Adair smiled. *Where am I sleeping as I dream this?* she thought. At home in Honolulu, she hoped. After all this awful cold, she wanted to wake up to some potent sunshine. *I'll have to try to remember all the details to tell Fletcher*, she told herself, looking around. What would he think of such an incredible dream?

"He'll tell me I shouldn't have had the *lau lau* for a late snack," she muttered, and Lilith glanced over at her. Adair just smiled and shook her head. Still talking to herself.

Darkness seemed to come early. Amazingly, none of them thought to bring a watch, and the batteries in the minister's shelf clock had run down long ago. But that was appropriate, as time was irrelevant here. They were literally in a state of suspended animation. Remembering how chained to the clock she had been while working at the bank, Adair thought this symbolic timelessness ironic.

When the darkness had grown to the point that Andi turned on the sanctuary lights, Cody snapped out of a light slumber. He stretched and groaned, "We still here? Man, I'm gettin' something to eat." He disappeared toward the kitchen.

The others seated around the auditorium then bestirred themselves to the kitchen as well. They tanked up as if for a twenty-mile hike, eating and drinking everything they could get their hands on. While there was enough to go around, by the time they were done eating, the kitchen was devoid of any food but half a box of the original Communion crackers. And the only reason those were left is they were slightly stale.

They washed up, Sophie pining for some toothpaste. "I'll sure appreciate seeing the Olympic-sized tub at Fletcher's house again," Adair admitted. "And the shower! He has this shower that sits out on the balcony—" She caught herself at their various amused and embarrassed expressions.

"Great. We'll come check it out," Cody said. Lilith tried to reprimand him, but snickered instead.

They settled down once more in the sanctuary to sleep. Holding Daniel close, Adair looked up at the windows in the darkness. Although she could not see them, she knew them well enough by now to picture them in her mind: Jesus at the door here, with the sheep over there, on the cross up front, and on the horse across from that. Knowing there was much more to them than she realized, she began to feel a vague desire to understand more about them—for instance, why she felt they were holding these walls up instead of vice versa. How could glass be stronger than stone? How could the tiniest spark of light slice through the thickest darkness?

Thinking of light, Adair raised her head toward the window of Jesus at the door. She should have seen the motel's lights painting the window, but it was as dark as the others. That must be due to whatever was happening outside now. Oh, well. That was outside. They were inside. Adair laid her head back down and closed her eyes.

She had almost drifted to sleep when she startled up, heart pounding. For a moment she thought she was back in her old apartment, sleeping, and the alarm was ringing. She thought the alarm was ringing and she was sleeping through it.

After coming fully awake, Adair realized she was afraid that if the train whistle sounded in the night when she was asleep, she might not hear it. She had always been such a sound sleeper that few things could wake her in the dead of night. Although one of the others would surely hear it and wake her, she did not feel she could leave the responsibility of staying alert to anyone else.

But then, what if she stayed awake all night listening and it came in the morning? She might be so tired by then that no one could wake her. What would poor little Daniel do?

For the first time since coming to the church, Adair was afraid. She didn't fear Darren or Sandra or anyone with the Warfield Group. The red slime couldn't fool her and the bogeymen from her past didn't spook her. She had every confidence in Fletcher's adequacy and trustworthiness. What she feared was herself—her own weaknesses that might prevent her following through on Fletcher's instructions. What if she slept through the train's coming?

As she sat gripped by this fear, she heard something. Clear and piercing, it sounded a clarion call that shattered her fears like flimsy glass. It was the whistle.

Adair jumped to her feet, hoisting Daniel. "Get up! It's the whistle! The train's here!" she exclaimed.

Daniel jerked upright. "The train! Daddy's train!" he cried happily.

There was an excited stirring, everyone scrambling for their coats in the dark. "Do you have Sphinx, Lilith?" Adair asked. The continued blowing of the whistle pumped her full of adrenaline.

"Mom? You got Sphinx?" Cody demanded in the dark.

"I . . . I decided not to go. I think I'll just stay here," Lilith said in a strange, high voice of fear.

"No way, Mom! Get up!" Cody ordered. He found her arm and yanked her to her feet.

"Here's the cat! I have her," Sophie said from Adair's left.

"Good. Andi, where are you?" Adair asked.

"Here. Beside you," Andi said in a breathless voice just behind her. The whistle blew again.

"Okay. That's everybody. Let's go." As Daniel clutched her neck, Adair led them down the aisle to the doors. With her breath coming in gasps, she reached out and opened the door.

She stepped out and stopped, the others crowding behind her. Now she saw why the motel's neon lights no longer painted the window. A sheet of thick red rain was pouring down from the black sky, sizzling and bubbling, obscuring everything with the mist it created. It splashed heavily off brickwork and gathered in a river that used to be the street. Beyond, Adair heard the crackling of numerous large fires. Despite them, the air was cold and heavy, reeking of the odor of the pits.

"We can't see where we're going! We can't get there!" wailed Lilith.

This certainly seemed to be the case—until the whistle blew again. The direction of its origin was clear. Shifting Daniel to her left arm, Adair said, "Yes, we can. We can follow the sound. Lilith, take my hand." She reached behind her, grabbing Lilith's sleeve and following it to her hand.

"I can walk, Mommy. I'm a big boy," Daniel said, sliding down from her arm to take her left hand.

"Good!" Adair praised him. "Sophie, you take Lilith's other hand."

"I have it," Sophie said behind her.

"Andi, take Sophie's hand," Adair instructed.

"But I'm carrying the cat," Sophie said.

"Give her to Cody and take Andi's hand," Adair said.

There was some rustling and then Andi's voice said, "We're linked up."

Straining against blindness, Adair said, "Okay, Cody, you take—"

"I got Andi in one hand and the cat in the other, so can we just dip?" Cody asked, agitated.

"Let's go then." Adair breathed deeply. Gripping Daniel's and Lilith's hands, she stepped out blindly into the red avalanche.

Although she could not precisely feel the flow against her legs, its pull was forceful. She had to brace against the sensation of a powerful current rushing around her. With the cold and the blindness, it was almost overwhelming. But she knew the others were behind her, depending on her to lead them, so she moved forward by feeling for the steps and sidewalk under her feet, guiding herself by scraping her shoulder continuously against the building.

When she came to a corner and didn't know where to go, she stopped. "What is it? Go on!" Cody shouted from behind.

"Be quiet!" Adair ordered. She waited, shivering, until she heard the whistle again, clearly to her right. She promptly turned the corner and went in that direction.

"What if they stop blowing it? If they stop blowing it, we're lost," Lilith moaned.

"Don't worry," Adair breathed, concentrating every particle of energy on listening to the whistle and placing her feet safely for the others to follow. The red stream that flowed down the street hit her somewhere around the knees—she couldn't tell because she couldn't feel it at all. The longer she walked, the less of an impediment it became.

Except that she still couldn't see. Walking blindly

through that hostile atmosphere was an unnerving experience—Adair could not tell if she might be leading the group into a ditch, a lamppost, or a parked car. Even curbs were formidable obstacles.

Then the whistle blew again, and it was so close it startled them all. "I see a light!" Sophie shouted.

Adair raised her face and promptly stumbled over the train tracks. "There's the platform! Right in front of you, Adair!" Cody called. She looked up into the headlight of the train, its vast hulk looming above them.

There was a mad rush for the platform steps. The porter, the same one who had assisted the Streikers off the train, appeared at the head of the steps. "All aboard! One at a time, please." Adair heard the clattering of footfalls on metal steps in front of her. Thrusting Lilith ahead, Adair saw the first few letters of the train's name emblazoned across the side of the car; M O If there were any doubts before, that dispelled them. It was the Morning Sun.

Then she was mounting the steps into the car with Daniel. Inside, they all stood blinking at each other in the light. When Adair's eyes adjusted, she took a quick tally: Daniel, Lilith, Cody, Andi, Sophie, and Sphinx. They were all here. They had all made it. Adair dropped down to a seat, crying in gratitude.

Lilith gathered up Sphinx and hugged her till she meowed loudly in objection. "Wow," Cody said. "Look out there."

From inside the train, they could see through the red deluge as if it were only a mist. Adair's mouth dropped open. "Someone else is coming!" she exclaimed.

They gathered at the windows, watching as a young mother with two small children stumbled toward the train. She ran blindly into a fire hydrant and fell. It must have hurt her, because she couldn't seem to get up. Adair watched anxiously, then turned to Daniel in the seat. "Wait right here," she ordered. He opened his mouth to protest fearfully, but she was already to the door of the car. She was going back out to help the others on.

As she started out, the porter blocked her exit. "I'm sorry, ma'am, but anyone who gets off the train cannot get back on. Please go to your seat and stay there."

Adair stared at him, then immediately returned to her seat. Daniel climbed onto her lap and hugged her in relief. Adair wrapped her arms around him, looking out in distress at the woman who had fallen so close to the train.

She was still down, her two children hovering in fearful confusion around her. But when the train whistle sounded again, she lifted her head and struggled up. Gripping their hands, she stumbled up over the tracks to the platform. In another moment she and her children were safely aboard.

Adair rushed to meet her. "I'm so glad you made it! How did you know to come? Did you see Fletcher?" she asked joyfully.

The little mother stared at her. "I loaded up the kids in the car to leave town, but we got stuck in the drifts. We was walking along back when we met up with this fella who told us to come to the train. He said if we wanted to leave, to listen for the train coming through," she explained softly, then ushered her children on back to another car.

Adair sank down in her seat. "We weren't the only ones," she whispered. "All that while he was working on getting other people out. And they didn't have to come to the church first! Oh, Fletcher—!"

Sure enough, they soon saw others making their

way to the train as the whistle continued to blow. Adair watched in rising excitement as people began pouring from the dark red streets toward the platform. She remembered Fletcher saying that the pits' overflow would be fatal—obviously, he meant to those intent on staying. But for those acting on his promise of safe transport out, it amounted to no more of a threat than a bad hair day. Being seated close to the door, Adair could see everyone who came on the train. She tried to count, but lost track at fifteen when a sudden rush of passengers flooded the aisle.

Suddenly Cody cried, "Case! There's Case!" He flipped the window latches to lower the large window and call out, "Case! Here! Case!" meanwhile waving his arms wildly.

Apparently Case never saw him or heard him, but made his way reliably to the platform anyway. As he appeared in the train car, Cody grabbed him and hugged him. "You made it! How did you make it?"

Case grinned crookedly. "That guy's coldblooded, man. He sprung me again and told me he was gonna mop me if I didn't get my gluteus maximus on this train."

Cody chortled and then Lilith gasped, "Powell! Powell Rodgers!" Several of them turned to stare at a thin, nervous man who had just boarded. "Powell, where is Daynell?" Lilith demanded. Ashamed, he ducked his head and darted back to another car.

Adair's head was spinning plenty by now, but the whistle was still blowing and more people were piling on. She didn't know what the capacity of the train was, but she felt sure that no one would be turned away for lack of space. Moreover, her friends knew many of those who were boarding and greeted them tearfully— there were Cody's friend Boone and his family, Joshua Potters, and Sheriff Guftasson, among others. But even those nobody knew found themselves congratulated on having made it to the train.

So there was general astonishment when, of all people, Gus Gramble appeared in the car. After exchanging open-mouthed stares with them, he mumbled, "I'm going to see my son."

"Good, Gus. Good for you," Adair replied quietly. He nodded awkwardly at her before hurrying on to another car. Watching him, Adair thought, *I knew there had to be a reason he kept showing up to harass us. He was really trying to reach Fletcher, to find out about his son! Well, it doesn't matter what motivated him to come, or how much he fought it. All that matters is, he's here now.*

Adair sank down into the seat, staring out the window. The fires raging across Beaconville were visible clear to the horizon. Watching them burn, she thought about the business owners who were too stubborn to relinquish control to the only person who could save them from this conflagration. All their stores would soon look exactly like Sophie's. Fletcher kept trying to tell them that. But . . . some listened. Some came—

"That's what he meant!" Adair cried, but in all the excitement nobody but Daniel paid any attention to her. "He said he was going to blow apart the Warfield Group, and look! All the people they had under their control blowing out of town! It's like—a big prison break!" she laughed to Daniel, who grinned because of her joy, not because he understood.

They kept coming, as the whistle kept blowing. In all this elation Adair saw only one discouraging scene. A young couple made their way all the way to the platform—the guy was even inside the car—when the girl said, "Well, we're here. I hope you're happy." She herself was still outside on the platform.

He turned around. "Aren't you coming?"

She snorted. "Where? Mister Rogers' Neighborhood? You crack me up."

"You said—" he floundered.

"I told you I'd get you here and I did. But you can't make me get on this train to nowhere," she said derisively.

"But—" he argued, torn.

She added icily, "Have a nice trip," and turned away.

"Wait! Heather, wait!" he shouted, jumping back off the train. Adair did not know what happened to them after that. She never saw either of them again.

"All aboard! Last call!" the porter warned. Adair got up from her seat to look anxiously out the window. She saw no one else coming through the streets toward the train. And as far as she knew, Fletcher had not yet boarded.

The whistle sounded again, one long, final warning. Then Cody shouted, "There he is!"

There was such a rush to the window that Adair couldn't see. "Fletcher? Do you see Fletcher?" she generally implored, straining to look over ten heads. The train's engine lurched into gear and they slowly began moving.

"You calling me?" he said.

Adair spun to see him hop up the steps just as the porter closed the door behind him. He was wearing his suede coat and the black Stetson she had given him for Christmas.

Adair was paralyzed by joy and relief, but Daniel cried, "Daddy!" hopping up on the seat with his arms outstretched. Fletcher caught him as the train lurched again on its way out of town.

"Fletcher." She fell on him and buried her face in

his coat. Since her lips were unavailable, he kissed the top of her head. Everyone else then crowded around him to thank him or grab his hand or just babble (as Lilith was doing).

He was smiling, trying to listen to everybody at once, when suddenly his face clouded and he said, "Shh!" Everybody went quiet.

Then they heard the faint cry, "Wait! Hey there— wait for me!" Looking out the window Cody had opened, they saw a man running alongside the moving train, waving for them to stop.

Adair gasped, "Carl! Fletcher, that's my father!"

≫ 14 ≪

Fletcher jumped to the window and shoved the pane all the way down, opening it wide. He tossed his hat onto the seat as he leaned down out of the window, reaching out to Carl. "Hurry! Grab my hand!"

He was only about five feet away, but the train was gaining speed. "I can't make it!" Carl panted.

"Yes you can!" Fletcher insisted. He sat on the window edge and leaned out precariously far, gripping the casing with his right hand while stretching his left to Carl.

"Stop the train!" Adair gasped, turning wildly to Sophie beside her. "Tell them to stop the train!"

"Not possible," Fletcher grunted, reaching hard.

"Ohh," Adair groaned in distress, leaning beside him to look down on her father. He was sweating and wheezing, his face pale and panicky as he reached up again and again, only to fall short of Fletcher's taut hand each time.

231

"I can't make it!" Carl cried. But before he could give up, Fletcher had dropped down even lower and seized his wrist. With an incredible surge of strength he hoisted Carl up to the open window till he fell halfway through.

For an agonizing instant they were suspended in a delicate balance, both of them half in and half out, facing opposite directions. But Carl, dissipated, tired, and weak, could not pull himself all the way in, and no one in the car moved fast enough to grab him. He began slipping out again.

In that instant Fletcher shoved him in from behind. The momentum thrust Fletcher from his tenuous position, and he fell out the window. In the next moment Carl was gasping upside down on the seat, and Fletcher was rolling on the ground beside the moving train.

"Fletcher!" Adair screamed, leaning out the window. "Fletcher!" Several pairs of arms held her from behind to make sure she did not follow him.

He scrambled to his feet and waved, growing smaller and fainter as the train gained speed. "Go on home, Adair!" he shouted. "I'll see you at home! Go home!" And then he had faded from view.

Stunned, she clung to the window until someone pried her hands loose and closed it. She wasn't aware that she had sat down until Daniel laced his little arms around her neck. "I'll get you home, Mommy. I'll call Spud and he'll fly us home," the little man said confidently.

She looked up at his precious face and slowly squeezed his belly. Sophie said quietly, "May I go back with you? I want to be there when he comes. I want to thank him myself."

Adair blinked. "Of course," she whispered, relaxing. Of course Fletcher could get himself home—he had means of traveling anywhere in the world. And he would come straight home now that the hard part was done: getting them out. There was no reason she should feel such a pain of parting.

She looked at her father as he bemusedly straightened himself on the seat beside her. "Unh," he grunted, reaching under himself to extract Fletcher's beautiful Stetson, crushed. Adair took it from his hands with a little cry of dismay. "Well. Never thought I'd make it," he said.

"You wouldn't have; you understand that? Do you understand that he fell out getting you in?" Adair asked, her voice rising.

"Sure, honey, sure," he said quickly, patting her knee. "Well. Let's see what they got to drink on this train." He gathered himself up and betook himself down the aisle to the next car.

Adair laughed shakily, hugging the ruined hat. "Oh, Fletcher, the projects you take on," she noted. She looked out the window, the ache heavy in her heart.

Daniel leaned against her, yawning. When he began struggling with his coat, she reached over to help him take it off. Then she saw that somehow, in the darkness and commotion at the church, he had tied Mr. Fuster around his waist with his blankie. Adair shook her head in amazement at his ingenuity. He pulled blankie loose and tucked it up to his face, contentedly stuffing Mr. Fuster under his head on her lap. "I can't wait to see Daddy," he murmured sleepily.

Adair leaned her head back as the train raced smoothly homeward. "Me neither," she whispered, drained. She looked around at the others, who had dropped into reclining seats to sleep.

Lights were turned off one by one, and Adair gazed out the window. What she saw now was a normal,

God-made landscape at night with rolling hills and quiet ponds. She saw the dark silhouettes of trees marching by in a stately parade, and above them, stars—a host of them, twinkling, dancing, pointing the way home. Breathing Fletcher's name, she closed her eyes.

*

A ringing sound woke her—an irritating ringing, ringing that wouldn't stop. Tossing her heavy head, eyes cemented shut, she mumbled, "Good heavens, that sounds just like that awful alarm clock I used to have." From old habit, she reached over and pushed something that made it stop.

She opened her eyes and looked around. She was in a bed. There were walls around the bed. She looked for Daniel by her side, but he was not there.

"Daniel!" She sprang up, wide awake. Then as she took in the familiar walls and the alarm clock and the accounting book open on the bed beside her, she felt a cold wash of dread.

"No," she whispered, slowly moving out from under the covers. She looked at the old, tacky carpet and the tiny bath off the bedroom. "No, it can't be!" she insisted. "Daniel!"

She stumbled out of the bedroom into the closet-sized living room of her old Wilderness Trails apartment. Looking at the morning sunlight filling the little kitchen window, she realized with a breaking heart that Daniel was not here. He had never been here. And Fletcher had been just a dream.

"No," she moaned, sinking to the hard, second-hand love seat. "It couldn't all have been a dream. It was too real! Fletcher is real. I know he is. I don't know what's going on, but I know it wasn't a dream!" she argued passionately.

She looked down at yesterday's newspaper scattered across the coffee table—Sunday, October 10. She raised her face. "Then today is Monday, the eleventh. The day Fletcher proposed through Charles Whinnet."

She got up to pace and think. "Maybe . . . maybe all that was a dream, but more than a dream. Maybe it was a premonition of what's going to happen. Maybe I will actually hear from Fletcher today." This encouraging supposition was clouded by the unfortunate fact that, apart from this vivid, expansive dream she'd just had, she'd never heard of any such billionaire.

Regardless, it appeared that she would have to actually get dressed and go to work today. It was an incredibly difficult transition to even think about, going from the freedom of life with Fletcher back to being a bank teller. Adair could not have forced herself to get ready without telling herself over and over that there must be a reason for all this. She *knew* it was not simply a dream. Fletcher was too real—she could picture every detail of his face—and Daniel, with his blankie and bunny—their house in Honolulu—his friends and family—"I did not make all that up. I don't have the power of imagination," she said firmly in her cramped, mildewed shower stall.

But the cold reality of *this* world would not be denied. There was her big thick accounting book, and the sheet of problems she had been laboring over last night. At the top of one sheet was the warning in her own handwriting: "TEST NEXT WEEK." There were yesterday's dishes in the sink and last week's clutter on the floor. And when she dressed, it was in the same old clothes that were hanging there before. No filmy muumuus or sequined denims. And however much she dug through her bureau drawers, there was no white silk lingerie. Of all the beautiful things Fletcher had bought her, that was what she missed most right now—that gorgeous white silk.

Adair stood frozen over the bureau, remembering Fletcher's touch on the silk and his appreciative smile. Her eyes filled with tears. "You can't leave me here like this, after making me love you. Fletcher, don't do this to me," she whispered. There was dead silence in response. Adair lowered her head and forced herself to dress out of a sheer survival instinct—if she sat there for long, she felt she would lose her mind.

At 7:30 she stepped out of her apartment door, carrying the thick accounting book to purportedly study during lunch. It was an old habit she resumed without thinking—she'd take the book to work, forget about it all day long, then take it home and forget about it there.

From the stairs outside her door, she looked down on her Mazda, parked in its same old slot. She trod heavily down the steps and stood over the car to survey the gash in the bumper where she continually hit the pylon. "My, won't Duane be surprised to see me there on time," she joked, sliding into the driver's seat. Then she momentarily collapsed in tears over the wheel.

Resolutely, she straightened and started the engine. "Something is going on. I don't know how to explain it, but it wasn't just a dream," she repeated, wavering between despair and determination.

Pulling out onto North Central Expressway, she noted from a sign across the freeway that it was already eighty-five degrees—a typical October day in Dallas. She glanced warily at a tailgater in her rear-view mirror as she turned on the air conditioner, feeling warm air blow from the vents. She sighed, "I'd love to have felt that yesterday—," then caught herself. Yesterday she was not freezing in Beaconville. She was sweltering *here*, as she had been every summer and fall for the last few years. Why couldn't she make herself believe that?

"But then—why was it so real?" she whispered. "It was more real than anything else that's ever happened to me—" She paused, passing Madame Prochaska's corner studio. Hadn't he given her ballet, then taken it away only to fill it with such greater significance before giving it back again? What meaning would dance ever have for her again without him?

Blankly, she turned into the parking lot of the Richardson branch of Two Rivers Bank. She hadn't seen any hurt animals on her way here, nor was she late. Slowly, eyeing the drive-through teller lanes, she got out of her car and carried her accounting book into the bank.

Courtney looked up as Adair came in and absently shoved her purse and book under the counter. "Hi," Courtney said with a chipper toss of her auburn curls. "Have a good weekend? I did. Jack took me to—"

"Courtney, who owns this bank?" Adair interrupted to ask.

"Huh? I dunno, some East Coast conglomerate," Courtney shrugged.

"Have you ever heard of Fletcher Streiker?" Adair demanded.

"No. Who's that?" Courtney asked, frowning. "Are you okay?"

"Not really," Adair said hollowly. She turned to the drive-through window as an early customer rolled up. "Hello. How are you?" she said, extending the mechanical drawer. While the customer handed over his deposit, Adair looked past his car for any motorcycles. There were none.

Courtney continued to stand at her elbow, telling her in monetary detail about the weekend with Jack. Adair tried to listen, knowing how important it was to have somebody listen, but she was relieved when Sergeant Charlotte scowled in their direction and Courtney had to start processing checks.

Against her will Adair resumed her regular life, settling into the quicksand of her old work routine despite the persistent inner denials: *I did not dream him up. Fletcher is real. He proposed to me. I accepted without ever seeing him. We got married with Charles standing in as proxy. Then I met him at the Galleria—*

"Adair?"

"What?" Startled, she inadvertently snapped at sweet little Sharon Betschelet, who had come up behind her unnoticed.

Sharon immediately retreated, murmuring, "Never mind."

At once Adair felt remorseful. Sharon had helped her more times than she could count, and here she was snapping at her like an alligator. But before Adair had any opportunity to apologize, Charlotte, the head teller, came up. "Adair, I need you on the lobby lines." She nodded firmly toward the crowd in the lobby. Lines of customers had materialized out of thin air, as if somebody had just announced that Cowboys tickets were on sale today.

Adair quickly opened another window and began handling payments and deposits. One young man handed her a soiled, wrinkled check for cashing. A glance at it told her it was no good—it was a rebate check for five dollars dated three months ago, made out to a "Julie Worrell," no less. He must have found it in the trash.

"I'm sorry," Adair said, glancing up. "I can't—" She broke off, staring at him. She had never seen him before in her life, but something about his face was eerily familiar. It was his expression—a look of fearful defiance, of desperation, that reminded her of Daniel when she had first encountered him as a neglected child.

"It's just for five dollars," he said tensely.

"I'm sorry; the check is outdated," she said as gently as she could, as if she were talking to Daniel.

He wiped his face and leaned closer. "Look, I need the money. I got to scrape together enough cash to get my bike outta the shop today or I got no job. It's just five dollars. I'm desperate and nobody'll give me a break. Nobody gives a damn."

In his pain and bitterness, Adair remembered with a shock Daniel saying, *Will you love me when I have a different face?*

She opened her mouth in astonishment. "Daniel?" she whispered.

The eighteen-year-old admitted, "My name's Brandon Wiles." But under the hard, wary face was the soul of an abandoned child.

Adair reached under the counter with one hand and opened her purse. She pulled out the lone bill in her wallet—her lunch money for the next three days—and shoved it across the counter to him. "That's all I have," she whispered.

He looked down at the ten-dollar bill in surprise, then slowly took it and shoved it into his jeans pocket. He turned away from the line without a word while Adair crumpled the worthless check and tossed it in the trash can at her feet. He looked back at her once, then walked on out.

"Stupid. That was stupid," she breathed to herself,

taking the next customer's deposit. She glanced up to see Sharon watching her talk to herself, and Adair cringed. Now she was way too embarrassed to apologize to her.

Crystal came up and nudged her, whispering, "Duane wants to see you in his office. I'll take over."

"Right. Okay," Adair said absently, abdicating the line to head for the branch manager's office. *At least he can't holler at me for being late today*, she thought, then caught herself with a gasp. *This is it! This is when he tells me that Charles Whinnet wants to talk to me!* Heart pounding, Adair knocked on Duane's door.

At his answer, she opened the door and casually asked, "You wanted to see me?"

"Uh, yeah, Adair." He glanced up over his wire-rimmed glasses and preppie shirt. "Sharon asked for you to help her prepare the monthly statements. I can't imagine why she thought of training you on that, but I told her she could get who she wanted. You'll start training with her today."

"Okay," Adair slowly responded. That is not what she was expecting to hear, either. "Uhh, did . . . Charles Whinnet ask to see me, by chance?"

Duane looked up in surprise. "The president? Why would he want to see you?"

"No particular reason," she murmured, turning out.

"Oh, Adair—"

"Yes?" She turned back quickly.

"Thanks for being on time today," Duane noted with only faint sarcasm.

"Oh. Sure," she said, and returned to the counter to relieve Crystal.

As she counted out traveler's checks to a customer, Adair tried hard to ignore Sharon puttering behind her. Knowing that Sharon had been kind enough to offer to train her on the statements made Adair all the more ashamed for being rude to her.

That customer left and Adair turned to the next. Then she gasped, "Sophie!" reaching out to grab her hand.

It was unquestionably Sophie—the delicately wrinkled face, the soft gray hair, the bright blue eyes—but she looked startled and then flushed. "Good heavens, no one's called me that for years." With a questioning glance at the stranger who knew her childhood name, she presented a check for cashing.

Adair leaned forward to whisper, "Sophie, don't you know me? Adair! We left Beaconville together last night!"

Sophie looked mildly disturbed. "Dear, I've lived in Richardson for almost twenty years. Can you cash this for me, please?" she asked delicately.

"Certainly." Adair blinked rapidly, taking up the check with the unfamiliar name on it. She blushed deeply over her rashness in accosting a perfect stranger. Obviously, Adair had seen her in the bank before, and her subconscious mind had reproduced Sophie's face in the dream. That's all. *I'm losing my mind*, Adair thought calmly, counting out the woman's cash. *This is what it's like to go insane*

"Thank you. Have a good day," Adair said without expression.

Sophie tucked the cash in her black patent purse and then paused, taking something else out. "Actually, now that you mention it, I did have a remarkable experience yesterday. This will explain it." And she handed Adair a little tract titled, *What It Means to Be Saved*.

"Thank you," Adair said automatically. She stuffed the tract under her purse without looking at it and

241

smiled hollowly at the next customer. "Hello. How are you today?"

She took care of twelve or fifteen customers over the next hour with only half her brain engaged. The other half was thinking, *It was just a dream. That's all. I just wanted things to be different so badly that I made up this—this billionaire figure to come save me and make things different. Fletcher does not exist outside of my own demented mind. My life will never be any better than it is now.* And she began to wonder why she should hang on to such an empty existence.

As she sent the last customer in line off with, "Thank you. Have a good day," she became aware that Sharon was standing beside her. Adair looked up, smiling tightly. "You needed something?"

"Yes," Sharon said pleasantly, tossing her limp brown hair. "Did Duane tell you about the statements?"

"Yes," Adair said.

"Okay. Come back to my desk and let's get started on them," Sharon said. She sounded quite a bit more confident than usual.

"All right, but—" Adair glanced at the clock, which said 11:40. "Um, I really need my lunch hour to study my accounting—we're having a killer test next week. Can we start on them after lunch?" It was just an excuse. Adair needed to go off by herself to contemplate her imminent insanity.

"That's fine," Sharon said. "C'mon back to my desk anyway for just a minute. I have something for you."

"Sure," Adair said blankly. She followed Sharon to her desk behind a partition of plants.

"I've noticed that you seemed to be, um, under some stress lately. I know it hasn't been easy for you, with Duane on your case all the time, so I want you to have this." Sharon picked up a thick white book and handed it to her.

"Uh—thanks," Adair stammered. A glance at the embossed white cover of the book told her it was a New Testament.

"I'm in a Bible study group that meets Tuesday nights. I'd like for you to come with me tomorrow night," Sharon said.

"Well—thanks, but—" Adair began spinning a refusal, handing the book back to her.

"Even if you don't come, keep the book. It's really different and I think you'd enjoy it," Sharon insisted.

Adair stared at her, wondering where timid, little Sharon found such assertiveness. "Uh, sure. Thanks. I'll think about it. The Bible study, I mean," Adair said, retreating to the counter at front. She shoved the New Testament underneath the counter next to her purse and accounting book, then jumped on the next customer who came in. As long as she was busy, she wouldn't have to talk to Sharon any more before lunch.

As soon as the minute hand touched twelve, Adair grabbed her accounting book and rushed outside to the courtyard. She couldn't get a hot dog as she usually did because she had given away her lunch money, but—no big deal. She just needed to get by herself to have a nice, quiet breakdown.

"Forget it," she told herself, sitting hard on a stone bench. "I just need to get into some numbers and forget it." So she flipped open her book and with some astonishment read: "Wake up from your sleep, Climb out of your coffins; Christ will show you the light!"

"What . . . ?" Flipping the book over to look at the cover, she slowly realized that she had mistakenly grabbed the New Testament instead of her accounting book.

She opened it to look again at the verse she had just read. "'Climb out of your coffin.' . . . Fletcher said something like that to me at the motel. . . ."

Then she looked across the page and read, "Husbands, go all out in your love for your wives, exactly as Christ did for the church—a love marked by giving, not getting. Christ's love makes the church whole. His words evoke her beauty. Everything he does and says is designed to bring the best out of her, dressing her in dazzling white silk—"

Gasping, Adair slammed the book shut. "White silk!" she whispered.

Almost fearfully, she opened the book to a different place and read: "I'm simply trying to point out that under your new Master you're going to experience a marvelous freedom you would never have dreamed of. On the other hand, if you were free when Christ called you, you'll experience a delightful 'enslavement to God' you would never have dreamed of. . . ." And she thought of her fearfulness in accepting Fletcher's proposal, only to find that being chained to him was the most liberating experience of her life.

Adair stared down at the book in utter bewilderment. And then a familiar voice whispered inside her, *This is my file folder, Adair.*

"Your—" she gasped, looking up at the sky. It was a pure blue sky, behind which was barely restrained an arsenal of love from shooting out in fireworks. "Your file folder . . . ?"

The reality of the world beyond her senses broke on her with a thunderclap. He was real. He had all the power and wealth of the world at his disposal. He had contacts in every city, every realm. And he loved her with such unreasonable passion that he used every conceivable means to get the message across to her—

to wake her up, to make her alive, to give her everything she had ever desired.

She jumped up from the bench to pace. "I knew I was dreaming last night! I *knew* what I was experiencing was just a—a rehearsal. But I *knew* the choice we made to get on that train was the most important choice we'd ever make . . . and . . . Sophie made that choice. . . ."

Hardly breathing, Adair sat down again with the book trembling in her hands. "It wasn't just a dream. You *did* propose to me, and you gave me a—a picture of what you're really like. Why didn't I ever see you that way before?" Strangely, when she tried to picture his face now, the image blurred like a badly focused photograph. The specifics of his features melted away. All she could remember was how beautiful he was, and how he smiled at her.

She looked up at the sky again, brilliant and searing. "You're there. You just had to go away for a while, didn't you? You wanted me to understand what to do while you're gone."

Adair looked around, then shut the book and got up. She walked quickly back into the bank, where she found Sharon still seated at her desk. "Sharon," Adair said, and she looked up. "I'd . . . I'd like to go to your Bible study. I need to go."

Sharon smiled, and Adair saw traces of sweet Sugar in her face—someone who could be a friend. "Great! I'll pick you up about six-thirty tomorrow night."

"Okay," Adair nodded tentatively. Her stomach tightened in hunger. She knew she needed to eat, but had nothing to buy lunch with. "Um, I guess we can go ahead and start on those—"

Crystal came up, interrupting, "Adair, somebody left this for you. I've got no idea where it came from." And she handed Adair an envelope with her name on it.

Raising a brow, Adair opened the envelope and pulled out a twenty-dollar bill. Wrapped around it was a note that said, "The Lord told me to give this to you." There was no signature, nothing to indicate whom it was from. It was just another anonymous employee carrying out the Boss's instructions.

Adair gulped, then turned back to Sharon. "I—um, I've got to go throw down a hot dog, then I'll come right back and we'll get started on those statements, all right?"

"Good," Sharon said.

Adair went back outside to look for the hot-dog vendor who roamed the complex. Plans flashed through her head—one of the first things she needed to do tonight was contact her mother and stepfather—it had been way too long. Also, she needed to see if she could find Carl. And drop the accounting—it just wasn't her calling.

She almost smiled, shaking her head. In one night nothing had changed—she still worked at a job she disliked; she still had no money (well, not *much*); she still had no roots. But in one night everything had changed. She had received a proposal from the richest Man in the world, and who knew where He might take her?

Adair stepped into the courtyard sunshine, enveloped by the love of her new Husband. Someday she would actually meet Him. Soon.

Epilogue

"So then after we all got on the train safely and you fell out getting my dad on, I dreamed that I woke up back in my old apartment in Dallas! It was horrible! There was my accounting book open on the bed beside me, and I had to get up and go in to work at the bank!" Adair related breathlessly.

Across the table, Fletcher shifted and glanced at the palm trees waving gently outside the floor-to-ceiling windows, shading them from the early-morning sun. "That would've been a nightmare for Duane," he murmured.

Housekeeper Nona leaned over the rattan table to pour coffee, muttering, "Lemme tell you my dream. I dreamed I got a raise."

"Dream on, *wahine*. Not with your son gambling the way he does," Fletcher said firmly.

Fingering her silk robe, Adair resumed, "But you did get Carl on the train, at the very last minute."

247

"Sounds likely. Carl's the type to wait until the last minute to make any significant decision. He still won't talk to any of my people," Fletcher noted.

Adair nodded, disturbed. That's what he had said in her dream. She began, "Well, anyway—"

A yellow furball came sailing through the air. Fletcher sat upright to catch it before it knocked his freshly filled coffee cup into his lap. "You keep throwing it, I'm gonna keep it!" he shouted.

Daniel skipped over to retrieve his property. "But he can fly! Mr. Fuster can fly!" he insisted, throwing himself onto Fletcher.

"Not without a license. Now put him up or I'll ground him permanently," Fletcher warned, surrendering Fuster. The bunny had a bright bandanna pinned around his neck for a cape.

Daniel cradled Fuster and took refuge with Adair, planting bony knees to climb up in her lap. Adair hugged him tightly. "The worst part of it was losing you. It broke my heart to wake up and find you weren't there," she said, rocking him.

"Adair, we've talked about this. He's going to start sleeping in his own bed," Fletcher said firmly.

"You're grumpy, Daddy. Go back to bed," Daniel ordered from the safety of Mommy's lap.

Fletcher briskly rubbed his face. "Uhn. Yeah, I didn't sleep very well last night. I was busy fishing a bunch of folks out of hell." He glanced sidelong at Adair. "I oughta be flattered that you would make me such a Godlike figure, but—gee, not even I could do all that."

"You can do anything, Daddy," Daniel asserted, skipping out to let Fuster practice his landings in another room.

Fletcher thought for a minute. "The train part was

interesting. Yvonne was just telling me yesterday about a Christian periodical she ran across called the Morning Sun. They haven't requested financing, but they'll go under if they don't get some prompt backing. And they publish stories nobody else'll touch." He looked around for the telephone.

Adair gazed down at the plate of passion fruit in front of her. "There was more to the dream. I dreamed Sharon Betschelet gave me a copy of the New Testament you had given me. I know I haven't read as much of it as I should, but I did read the part where it said . . . it was really strange, but you know the passage about our relationship to God being like a husband-wife relationship? When I read that earlier, it just went in one eye and out the other—"

Fletcher's brow wrinkled in amusement and she amended, "You know what I mean—it didn't really sink in until the dream. There was a lot about God I thought I understood, when I really didn't." She thought about the windows in the church, and how lifelike they became the more she looked at them. There was a similar window in the church Fletcher had attended as a child here in Honolulu.

He studied her for a moment. "We still have time to make the early service, if you're willing to go. Desirée isn't bringing Charity over until this afternoon."

She looked up at his tan face and his soft brown eyes, remembering how it felt to think she had lost him. Then she knew there was Someone infinitely more beautiful she was in danger of losing. She had to get on that train. "Yes," she nodded. "I'll go."

"Good." He stood up, calling, "Daniel! Come upstairs! We need to get ready!"

Daniel scampered in from the next room, and they began up the spiral staircase. "There was so much more," she murmured. "I dreamed about that white silk you got me."

"Tell me all about that part," he said quickly, below her on the stairs.

She laughed, then demanded, "Hey, where's the Stetson I got you?"

He winced. "Oops, you noticed. I'm afraid I accidentally left it in Dallas. I'm not used to wearing a hat."

She tsked him. "Oh well, at least it's not ruined. It got ruined in my dream." Reflecting further, she thought about Sophie, and her heart broke a little to remember how much that lovely woman wanted to see Hawaii. Did Sophie really exist somewhere? If she did, Adair felt sure she would see her again, as they were both headed for the same destination.

At the top of the stairs, Adair urged Daniel into his room. "Adair," Fletcher said thoughtfully, and she turned, glancing with a smile at his bright print shorts. "What if it is just a dream? What if you're dreaming me now?"

Her immediate reaction was, *Don't wake me up.* But then she paused at a new turn of thought. "I think," she said, "this life *is* a dream, and I've been given a beautiful one. Someday I'll wake up to something even better. So as long as I'm dreaming, I guess I'd better dream up some way to thank Him."

Fletcher smiled.

To the Reader

A good allegory can be fun but dangerous if it lends itself to strange interpretations that the author never intended. For those readers who want to know what I had in mind writing the Streiker books, I offer the following clues (besides the more obvious scriptures already mentioned elsewhere):

On Fletcher
Song of Solomon 5:9-16
Psalm 18:11
Psalm 34:8
Psalm 36:7-8
Psalm 50:10-12

On Adair and Fletcher
Psalm 37:7
Psalm 63:1-8
1 Thessalonians 1:4
1 Peter 5:7

On Darren Loggia
1 Peter 5:8

On Fletcher in Beaconville
Psalm 139:8
Isaiah 28:15-18
Matthew 16:18
Ephesians 4:8-9
1 Peter 3:19
1 John 3:8b

On Adair and Friends in Beaconville
Zechariah 9:11-12
Ephesians 2:1-3

On Sophie
Ephesians 2:4-6

On the Windows in the Church
Revelation 3:20
John 10:14,27
Colossians 2:14-15
Revelation 19:11

On Sphinx the Cat
Romans 8:19-21

On Adair After Beaconville
Malachi 4:2

This short list does not begin to cover the analogous points I intended to make, and readers have found other significant parallels that had not occurred to me. Anything you find that is meaningful to you and is consistent with Scripture is acceptable to me.